The
Education
of
Mary

A Little Miss of Color, 1832

Ann Rinaldi

JUMP AT THE SUN
HYPERION BOOKS FOR CHILDREN
NEW YORK

For all my grandsons,
Michael, Phillip, Daniel, Patrick, and Ronald III

Printed in the United States of America
First Edition
1 3 5 7 9 10 8 6 4 2

Visit www.jumpatthesun.com
The text for this book is set in Goudy 13/16 pt.

Library of Congress Cataloging-in-Publication Data
Rinaldi, Ann.
The education of Mary : a little miss of color, 1832 / Ann Rinaldi.
p.   cm.
Summary: In 1832, Prudence Crandall begins admitting black girls to her exclusive
Connecticut school, scandalizing white society and eventually causing her arrest and the clos-
ing of her school.
ISBN 0-7868-0532-3 (trade)—ISBN 0-7868-2463-8 (lib.)
[1. Race relations—Fiction. 2. Prejudices—Fiction. 3. Schools—Fiction. 4. Racially mixed
people—Fiction. 5. Afro-Americans—Fiction. 6. Connecticut—Fiction.] I. Title.
PZ7.R459 Ed   2000
[Fic]—dc21   99-57621

The
Education
of
Mary

Prologue

In all stories there is a hero or a heroine. That's the notion I always had when I was little. And then I grew up and learned that you can go your whole life, which is certainly a story, and never meet one.

And then too, sometimes you have to be your own hero or heroine. This is a tiresome business at best, with the most awful part of it being that you never get to feel like one.

The only thing more dolorous than all of that, is suspecting that someone you came close to hating all your life is truly a hero or heroine. That can truly befuddle you. Sometimes at night, when my body is twitching so much from the din and the work in the mill here in Lowell, so much that I think I'm still dashing to tie up a broken warp thread or thread the shuttle, I cannot sleep. I get out of bed in the cold, wrap a blanket around me, and light a candle at a nearby table. Then I try to write notes about what happened to me in the last year or so. But I can never seem to sort it out. It's as if I have just one end of a broken warp thread and need the other end to tie it up.

But this night is different. This night, as I look around me at the huddled shapes of the other girls in their meager beds, hear the rasping of their uneven breathing, their coughing, even as I envy them their fitful sleep, I sense a new thought taking hold. More than a thought, it is a revelation creeping through me. What? What? Oh, I know I'll feel like the hind wheels of exhaustion in the morning, but I must pursue it. I must pay it mind.

And then it seems as if I have a purchase on it. Quickly, I must write it down by the light of the flickering candle. Yes, that is it!

Sometimes people do the most wonderful things for the worst reasons. Reasons you wouldn't want to be privy to because they are so removed from the good act done.

Somehow I think this is the other end of the broken warp thread I have been looking for, to make sense of my story. I put down my pen and feel elation at my discovery. As much elation as I feel when I bank my wages every week for my education. Now I will be able to write my story, bit by bit in odd moments stolen from this arduous life. Now I will measure out my words as I measure out my hard-earned wages that will, with the help of the money from my brother Charles, get me away from this desolate mill town with its brick boarding-houses and tenements and air so filled with soot you don't know half the time if it's night or day. But it's night, always night for us girls who are blasted to life by the factory whistles at four-thirty in the morning. I look back at those sun-filled days in Canterbury, Connecticut, and I think, which is real, here or there? And I know if I write it down, I will soon know.

Chapter One

—————◈—————

I was thirteen when I first started to work for Miss
Prudence Crandall at the Canterbury Female Seminary.
And it was not my idea. I was asked to help out. I'm not
one who easily believes in causes.

Back then the seminary was full of young white ladies of
eminence in fancy bonnets. They were all so high-toned that
I melted into the wall when they swished by me on the stair-
way in their dresses that were made especially for swishing.

They were better than I was. It was nothing that was my
fault. I was sensible of that. It was determined to be thus by
forces outside our circle of hopes and prayers. Mama said it
would someday change. Mama is a good woman, but I did not
believe her.

Never could I be like all those Amys, Phoebes, and
Hannahs.

My chores at the seminary were not tedious. I fetched for Miss
Crandall her pen, her ink, her writing paper. I accompanied
her on errands and carried her bundles. I made her tea. No small

accomplishment, for she insisted the blue cup that came from Holland be made hot first and the tea poured just right. And if I got any in the saucer, she made me start over again. To say Miss Prudence Crandall was not a stiff-necked Quaker lady was not to do her justice.

I came directly after school and on Saturdays. One day I must have acquitted myself especially well. "Mary," she said, "I don't know what I would do without you."

Don't think that didn't make me proud.

Then she smiled. "Mary, I wish you could be about all day. Do you think your father would let you come mornings and stay?"

"I have school, ma'am." I went to the dismal district school, with the poorer whites.

She nodded and sighed. Then she smiled again. "You could learn here. On the quiet. I could teach you. I shall write a note to your father and ask him. Would you like that?"

Would I like it? No more taunts from brother William, who thinks just because he's near fifteen, he can boss me around? No more finishing chores for sassy Olive, eleven, who's always running off to play? No more having to worry about Oliver and Benjamin who are eight and six? No more having to help sixteen-year-old sister Celinda with the dishes? No more having eighteen-year-old Sarah tell me to study harder. Be around Miss Crandall all the time? In this stately house on the town green, this house with the shiny heartpine floors and the Persian carpets?

"I would be most happy," I said.

And so she asked my father, a man so taken with education that I think he would have said yes to Beelzebub himself if he promised to aid his children's learning. He came to America from the West Indies so he could go to school and learn. It did not work out for him that way, and so now he wanted his children to learn. Wanted it with a burning that consumed him inside.

My father said yes.

Teach her on the quiet, he said. Teach her in the cellar, teach her in the attic, he cared not. Just teach her Latin and French and geography and sums and history and how to behave like a lady. What the agreement was between them I do not know. I kept doing my chores at the seminary and Miss Crandall taught me in her room, away from the others.

That is how it started in the fall of 1832 in our town of Canterbury, the experiment that caused Miss Crandall to become known not only in the county of Windham in Connecticut, but all over the country and the world. People think it started because of my sister Sarah, but she came to the seminary a month after I was already there and learning.

You see, we are people of color. Not much color, we girls, at least myself and Sarah and Celinda. Because we are all part Negro, part Indian, and part white, thanks to Daddy's background, Sarah and Celinda and I have only a small portion of Negro fluid in our veins.

How peculiar that Sarah, who is the most white, fought the

hardest for the Negro race. When people think of what happened at the seminary, it is her name they speak, not mine. She is their heroine. But people know only what is written in dark ink by dark-visaged men in the court records and newspaper accounts. Sarah's name is in the records. Mine is not.

Nobody even remembers I was there. Sarah and I are estranged now because of this, where before we were friends. There is nothing worse than the enmity that can fester between sisters.

Oh, how tainted with vanity she became because of the role she played. You could never convince her that she wasn't Joan of Arc in the flesh. When we were both attending the seminary but still living at home, she no longer fed the chickens or did the dishes. She sat on a fine cushion and read Chaucer. Her nose was so far in the air I'm surprised some bees didn't make a nest in it. "How can I ask her to wash dishes?" Mama said. "Why, she's so intelligent. A blessing of creation. She's got a calling to be a teacher!"

Funny thing, this calling. Sarah never heard it before I started at Miss Crandall's seminary. Then she heard it loud and clear like Gabriel's horn. Well, I shared a room with the Blessing of Creation. And I can tell you she snored.

Truth to tell, Mariah Davis started learning on the quiet there before either of us. Mariah worked at the seminary as a family assistant. That was Miss Crandall's fancified word for servant. Oh, Miss Crandall did have her ways. Mariah lived down the road and was betrothed to my brother Charles. One day she asked Miss Crandall if she could slip into classes and listen after she was done with her chores. Miss Crandall said yes. And none of the Phoebes or Amys or Hannahs cared a whit. Everybody likes Mariah because she meets people on common ground.

My sister Sarah doesn't meet anybody anywhere. All the ground is hers, all the time, and she's always looking for more. Difficult for me to think that I once looked up to her so, before any of us went to the seminary. Difficult and painful. I remember just how it came to be that she started at the seminary. I remember the night she started getting notions.

My daddy's farm was not doing well that year of 1832. There had not been enough rain, the crops were stunted, and people were holding on to their money. Everybody feared a panic, which, while not good for white folk, is always worse for people of color.

Sarah was near betrothed to George Fayerweather, a respected blacksmith. His family went all the way back to before the Revolution. "To the great years of the Narragansett plantations," Sarah pointed out. His family came from Rhode Island.

Sarah had been working as a servant in the elegant home of Mr. Jedediah Shephard. She wanted more. Sarah knew there was more, as we all did. I suppose I cannot really fault her.

My brother Charles, the oldest at twenty-one, was an agent for *The Liberator*, a newspaper for colored folk owned by that man Garrison. My daddy would have much rather Charles had taken to farming, and wouldn't have the paper in the house. Mariah loved that paper, though, and took her copy to the school. Mariah and Sarah were friends and Sarah often visited her at the seminary. And so it came to be that Mariah showed *The Liberator* to Sarah. Wars have been started, I am given to understand, with as little provocation.

The weather was hot enough to stretch the day beyond endurance so that a measure of insanity seemed to take hold. I had worked in the fields with the others after school until sundown. The timothy, oats, and barley had to be cut, the apples and pumpkins picked, the cows milked. Then my sister Celinda and I made the supper and helped get the little ones, Oliver, Benjamin and four-year-old Jane Elizabeth, to bed.

Sarah and I often spoke in the darkness before going to sleep. I learned a lot from her. She was quick. But this night, the dark space between our beds seemed to be distilled with something I could not name, like something in the very air was changed.

"I'm tired of working the fields," Sarah said. "We need to do headwork, not labor. For two hundred years the Americans have practiced nothing but headwork. And we have done their drudgery. Is it not time for us to imitate their example and practice headwork, too?"

All I wanted to do was sleep. "I consider myself American," I mumbled. "And the drudgery we do is in Daddy's fields, remember. Not in someone else's like our brethren in the South."

"Our color is held in contempt, and by doing labor we perpetuate the feeling."

I raised my head. "Has the heat made you sickly? Shall I fetch Mama?"

"I am sick of the hypocrisy that mocks the truisms of American society. Such hypocrisy claims that all men are born equal excepting those whose hair is woolly."

"Your hair is not woolly, Sarah. Nor is mine. We're near white, both of us, and Celinda."

"I'm sick of being a bond servant."

"You get paid by Mr. Shephard. A bond servant does not," I reminded her.

"I am in bondage all the same. We all are. Mary, Miss Crandall's been teaching you all along on the quiet. I wonder what would happen if a girl of color asked to attend classes?"

"Mariah already does," I reminded her.

"She's a servant. I mean, I wonder what would happen if a girl of color walked up that front walk and asked to be admitted into that fine green door with the fanlight overhead."

My sleep had fled. Since Miss Crandall had been instructing me, Sarah had passed several remarks. Said things like "uppity." And "Miss Fancy Pants." And "You sure you want to break humble bread at this table with us?" I had thought she was teasing.

"I think," I said carefully, "that learning is learning if you go in the front door or the back." You had to be careful with Sarah. Careful not to get on her wrong side. She was like a viper if you crossed her.

"You think if I asked her, she would say yes?" she pushed.

No sense in lying. "Most likely."

"What makes you so sure?"

"Because she is a Quaker and has a Christian conscience, like her ancestors. She told me how one of them burned at the stake in England in 1555 for refusing to renounce his Protestantism."

"Perfect," she sighed.

"Sarah, don't ask her. You'll ruin everything for me and Mariah!" I begged her.

But Sarah did not care about me or Mariah. She wanted nevermore to work the fields or clean house for Mr. Shephard. And she had found her way.

That week she kept the candle burning in our room, devouring back issues of *The Liberator* she'd sneaked into the house. I learned more about slavery than I needed to know. "Ten thousand families in the South own more than fifty slaves each," she would tell me. Or: "There is a slave auction in front of the nation's Capitol."

She'd tell me about William Lloyd Garrison. "His paper gives a voice to women, both black and white! He calls himself a peace-disturber, a fanatic, even a madman!"

I was angry because she was robbing me of my sleep. She had to talk to somebody about all this. And she wasn't sure yet how George Fayerweather would receive it. George bragged about how, in 1767, Parson Fayerweather christened his servant man, George's ancestor, giving him his name before a large congregation in his church. Never mind that that ancestor was a slave.

"I tell you, Mary, this man would be behind a girl of color getting a good education. The time and the circumstances are right. Someone has to step forward."

I should warn Miss Crandall, I told myself. But I didn't. Within the week Sarah had given her the full benefit of her passion. Mariah and I listened in the hall.

"I do not wish to sit on the floor, or get taught on the quiet like my sister Mary. I wish to attend classes seated at a proper desk, with pen and paper in hand. Please, Miss Crandall, I don't want to 'forever be a sojourner in the dwelling of my master,'" she begged.

"You quote Alexis de Tocqueville," Miss Crandall said.

"Yes, he is a favorite of mine."

Miss Crandall was befuddled, a state of mind to which she was not usually prone. "The Board of Visitors expects me to elevate this school to the level of the female academies in Norwich, Litchfield, and Hartford," she told Sarah.

"'They have sold us in their marketplaces like cattle,'" Sarah said. "'They have driven us in large droves from state to state, beneath a burning sky.'"

"Now you quote Mr. Garrison." Miss Crandall felt herself at a distinct disadvantage.

"'They have lacerated our bodies with whips. They would destroy our souls.'"

All this talk of whips and destroying souls was too much for

Miss Crandall. We heard her sigh. "When I took the job as director, my brother Reuben wrote to me: 'Remember you were baptized a Baptist. Not by a sprinkling, but by full immersion in the Quinebaug River. I sincerely hope you will use discretion in all your undertakings.'"

"Miss Crandall, I have heard you say that one person's discretion can be another person's failure," Sarah made bold to say.

Silence. Then Miss Crandall spoke. "Give me time. I shall think on it."

Sarah's request did give her pause. For a whole week she walked around with a peculiar look in her eyes. Several times I caught her reading *The Liberator*. Then she called her household help together to tell us she'd had her "conversion." She said yes to Sarah.

"I will not come if it will injure you in any way," Sarah said. Though I know she would willingly injure Miss Crandall, herself, Mariah, me, and even the cows eating the nubbins in the fields, if she could, to further her own aims.

"As a true Quaker, Miss Harris, I must come to the aid of the oppressed. If I am injured on your account, I will bear it," Miss Crandall said.

Chapter Two

"**D**o you want to do this thing, Sarah?" my daddy
asked her that night.

"Yes, Daddy."

"If you do, you must get your education and not cause trouble."

"All I want is an education, Daddy. It's what you wanted for
all of us, isn't it? Now here is my chance. Surely you won't
deny it."

I had to admire the way Sarah could bring Daddy around.
She knew his sadness at his own lack of learning ran like a
dark undertow through him, sometimes pulling him into
bleak moods. She knew that even after he was well placed
enough so that Mama didn't have to work in the house of
Huldah Kinne anymore, he still made her go there. Because
Huldah Kinne taught Mama to read.

"And so you shall do this thing, then, daughter," he said.
"So you shall."

So Sarah not only started at the school, she came up that
front walk and knocked on that dark green front door every

day just like Miss Smart Boots, sassy as can be. And she wasn't above pausing before entering and twirling her parasol and nodding to any elite ladies who happened to be walking on the green. She walked on those Persian carpets like she was out of the ancient Hebrew scriptures. Esther in calico. And she learned to swish her skirt with the best of them.

Mariah and I still went through the back door. I still got taught on the quiet. Mariah still sat on the floor in back of the room after her chores were done.

For that whole first week Miss Crandall went around saying that people like Mariah and Sarah were in bondage.

If you ever laid eyes on Mariah you'd wonder if Miss Crandall hadn't taken leave of her senses. Mariah is tall, stately, beautiful, and proud. She looks like some queen from Angola, out of place here in the Connecticut countryside. She has a mouth on her too and isn't above using it on my brother Charles. But then, I would venture to say that brother Charles sometimes needs it.

But Mariah in bondage? It made me laugh.

Sarah insisted on going home nights. Sitting in class with the Phoebes, Amys, and Hannahs was one thing. Sleeping in the same room with them was another. Still, all that first week I worried.

"Someone is going to complain about your being there," I told Sarah in the dark of our room. "Maybe Mr. Judson, the lawyer who lives across the green from the seminary."

"Let him knock on the door and complain," she said.

"Don't you see? It will ruin everything. Not only for me and Mariah, but maybe even for the rest of the girls."

"What do I care about those lily-white snobs? They can go to any school they want."

It was then that it first came to me. This was just as much a challenge to Sarah as it was a means of bettering herself. "Mariah and I can't," I said.

"Oh. And I suppose you and Mariah like sneaking around to get your education! Don't you know I'm doing this for you and her? And for your children?"

"I don't see why you have to bring my unborn children into it. I know you're smart, Sarah. I could never be as smart as you. But couldn't you just as well learn on the quiet, too?"

She sat up. She relit the lamp and got out of bed. She began pacing in bare feet on the cold floor. "Did it ever occur to you, Mary Harris, that sometimes we just have to stand for something in life? Believe in something?"

I must admit, it had never occurred to me. In a large family you're usually too busy surviving every day. "I go to church. I believe in God."

"I'm not talking about going to the Congregational Church in Westminster because we aren't allowed in the one in Canterbury. I'm talking about preserving the Union by removing an evil."

I felt suddenly ashamed. I had never given serious thought to preserving the Union.

"I know it's hard," she went on, "to believe in anything

when you see Mama so burdened by work. When you know what awaits the little ones. You ride, one more time, sister Mary, on top of the stagecoach in the rain because people of color are not allowed inside, and tell me you don't need something to believe in."

"All you get when you believe is hurt," I said.

"Who told you that?"

"Celinda."

She shook her head. "Celinda has no aspirations other than to work in the mills in Lowell. How many times did you see her waiting out there in the heat for the wagon that fetches girls to work at the looms in Massachusetts, and remain standing while they take the white girls and leave her behind?"

"Lots," I admitted.

"Yet every time she hears that stagecoach is coming she goes out there and stands, like a mule in the sun. Thinks if she stands there long enough things will change. Well, things don't change, Mary! You have to make them change. You have to have a part in it. You have to believe in something. And not be afraid of getting hurt."

"And what about if you hurt others along the way?" I asked quietly.

She shrugged. "Then they get hurt," she said. And she blew out the candle and got back into bed.

I lay quietly, thinking. What had come over Sarah? Certainly it wasn't the influence of quiet, gentle George Fayerweather, who bragged how his slave ancestor was given his master's name in church. *The Liberator*, I decided. It's like someone's been pouring hot lead into her brain every since she started reading it.

"Celinda said one of these days she's going to put down that she's white on that paper," I told her. I was testing her. My voice floated in the dark.

"The stage driver who picks up girls for the mills wouldn't take her. He knows her."

"Stephen Coit at the store has a friend who works for the mills. He's going to tell Stephen when they change drivers. And Stephen will tell me. And I'll tell Celinda."

"Why should Stephen do that for you?"

"Because he's my friend. And he buys Daddy's produce."

"Don't trust him. Don't trust any white man." She punched her pillow. "And that isn't the way to go about things. Celinda would be living a lie. She'd have to pass on that lie to her children. I intend to pass on something more to mine." She rolled over and in a short time I heard her snoring.

That was not a good time for people of color. Less than a year before, a slave preacher in Virginia name of Nat Turner crept into his master's house with his followers and killed the whole family while they slept. They killed seventy white people in all before the rebellion was squashed.

Mariah had told us about this. White folk in Canterbury

didn't speak of it at the time, but you saw it on their faces when you passed them on the street, the fear, the caution when a Negro approached. It was not a good time to be Negro.

"The only reason Miss Crandall took you into her school," Celinda told Sarah one day, "is because you're so light-skinned nobody will notice. She'd take me if I asked. But not Olive. Or little Jane Elizabeth. They're too dark."

What followed was the nearest thing to a rage that I have ever seen possess Sarah. She insulted Celinda, she cried, she stormed. And she quoted everybody from Thomas Paine to Anne Hutchinson. She threw around words like "mawkish sentiment" and "political hypocrisy," words I know meant nothing to Celinda. Then she told her she hoped Celinda did get hired at the cotton mills, so she could be a wage slave. That it was all she deserved.

Daddy brought an end to it. He hushed them both and sent them from the kitchen, though he held on to Sarah's hand a little, letting her know he favored her. Oh, how I wished I could do something to make Daddy hold on to my hand like that.

With Sarah's decision to be admitted to the school as a real student, something had come alive in Daddy again. Something none of us had seen in him for a long time, a light in his eye, a smile on his lips. "Bless that girl," Mama said. "I never thought I'd see him so happy again."

I was becoming downright jealous. He hadn't acted like

that when Miss Crandall asked him if she could teach me on the quiet. Was it because Sarah was flouting the natural order of things? How would he feel if Sarah's efforts were thwarted?

Of course he knew he could trust Miss Crandall. Hadn't he sold her milk and vegetables all these years? Before that he'd sold them to Mr. Paine, who'd owned the house before her. And it was Daddy who'd found Luther Paine, fallen down dead from chopping wood in his backyard.

Another time he'd been there when a white carpenter working for Mr. Paine fell from a ladder and got killed. When Daddy got in one of his moods, he said the Paine mansion was haunted.

I went about my business. But my jealousy of Sarah grew every day as I sat in a lonely room above stairs at school and she walked right into the classrooms and sat down with the Phoebes, Amys, and Hannahs.

"Why don't you make my sister use the back door?" I asked Miss Crandall that first week.

"Well, now, we don't want to make it appear as if we are hiding anything, do we?" she said.

Why, I wondered briefly. After all, she had hidden me. What was so different about Sarah?

Those last days of September passed by in a lull of warmth and haziness while bees droned outside the windows, the cows finished off the corn nubbins in the distant fields, and the leaves suffused the very light around us with a color that was not real.

On the last day of September I went to Stephen Coit's store for Mama as I did at least once a week. It was a pleasant chore. Stephen Coit had been a student of Miss Crandall's when she'd taught in Plainfield just across the river. His father was the sheriff. He was tall and thin and smart.

Because all kinds of people came into his store, he knew all the gossip. He wore spectacles and a clean white apron all the time. His store smelled of spices and pickles and coffee. He sold everything from harnesses to ladies' mitts. An uncle who lived in Boston made sure he was supplied with fresh lemons at all times, as well as many other delicacies that came in off ships at the Boston wharves. And he treated me like a grown-up. This is important when at home you are treated like a child.

That morning as he put the items in my basket, the fresh coffee beans, a bag of tea, a sack of flour, a cone of sugar, he smiled at me. "Tell your sister that the stage coming through tomorrow from the mills has a new driver," he said.

My heart leaped, then fell. That meant Celinda would be leaving! I must hurry home and tell her so she could pack. "Thank you, Stephen," I said. I paid my bill and took my leave. That would show Sarah about trust. And friendship. As I left he gave me some candy. Taffy. "For you," he said. He always gave me candy when I left. "Wish Celinda luck for me," he said. He'd gone to school with her here in the village as a child. Celinda's schooling had ended here in the village. He'd gone on to Plainfield. Always he asked after Celinda and on several occasions he'd told me how smart she was. Smarter than Sarah even, he said.

Celinda and I were doing the supper dishes. Sarah was sitting on the front porch with George Fayerweather. "You're going to be doing this chore tomorrow night by yourself. I hope you won't be sorry you helped me leave," Celinda said.

"I couldn't have done it without Stephen."

"He's a good person. Make sure you thank him for me. And keep him as a friend. He knows people at the mill and can always get word to me if you wish."

I nodded as I wiped the dishes. I liked Celinda. In so many ways she was more comforting to talk to than Sarah. She had sense and steadfastness. I think I even liked her more than Sarah. But when I got tired of sense and steadfastness, I needed Sarah, her passion, her dreams. To Celinda, dreams were something you had when you were asleep. My sisters were rivals, and I was caught in between, being a little of one and a little of the other. Often one complained to me about the other.

"I'm going to miss you, Celinda," I said.

"I know. But we can write. Now remember, you must promise not to tell anyone I'm leaving tomorrow. Not Mama or Daddy. And don't tell that I've put myself down as white when they discover I'm gone. Daddy will be shamed."

I promised and put my arms around her tall wiry frame, trying to keep from crying. She hugged me back. "You can walk with me to the stage stop. It's on your way to school. Only promise you won't tell anybody. And don't let Sarah lead you astray."

Early on the morning of October 1, Celinda and I left the house before anyone was up. I put up coffee on the stove for the family, helped her gather some ham, day-old biscuits, and apples into her knapsack. She carried a flimsy portmanteau tied with a rope and wore her Sunday cloak.

We waited in the wet, silent dawn while birds perched on fence posts around us and smoke curled up from chimneys in distant houses. "I've left a note for Mama and Daddy. You must make it right for me with them," she said. "I'm fearful they won't forgive me. But I can't stay here any longer. I don't want to work the fields or be a servant any more than Sarah does."

"I'll try," I said.

"You know Sarah's their favorite, don't you?"

I shrugged. "Why?"

"The first girl. The princess. The dreamer. The promise. So pretty. What she's doing now, going to that school, I can't keep up with that. Don't want to. And they expect so much from us, the light-skinned ones. Expect us to go far. You know that, don't you?"

I didn't answer.

"I just hope it works out and she don't break everybody's heart."

"Well, I'm going, too."

"Isn't the same in their minds as Sarah, going right in that front door." She laughed. "She is something. Got to give her credit. But look, you go on as you are, getting your education on the quiet. You're smart. Don't throw this chance away. And don't let it ruin you, either."

I scowled. "How could it ruin me?"

"Things go like sour milk, it could turn you on education."

"How could they go like sour milk?"

She frowned. "When the people in this town find out they will raise the Devil's own fuss. You know that Dr. Andrew Harris who lives across from the school? Well, I heard he's got his heart set on being governor and that's why he pushed Miss Crandall to open her school. Because it would be home to daughters of fancy important men in Connecticut. You think he's going to stand for sister Sarah being there?"

"No," I admitted.

"Isn't because I'm jealous of her, I say this. Hope all does go well. But if it doesn't, if it turns sour, you don't turn from education. Hold fast to what you know. We all must do what we must do to survive. Sarah has her way and I, mine. Here comes the stage." She picked up her portmanteau. "I'll write to you, Mary."

The stage was upon us, raising dust, horses neighing, harnesses rattling. The man on the driver's box looked down at us with all the authority of God on Judgment Day. Celinda handed up her paper. He took his sweet time about studying it. Time in which I felt God Himself brooding on us. And at that moment I wouldn't give a pinch of snuff for Celinda's chances. "They told me there was a nigra girl here who kept trying to get on at this stop. What happened to her?"

"I suppose she gave up trying, sir," Celinda said.

He gestured that Celinda should get in. She did, smiling at me. "I'm the only one riding, so far. Got the stage all to myself, like a grand lady," she said.

I don't know if that morning Celinda sensed she was leaving home for good. But I felt it. My heart felt as if it was being torn out of me. The driver whipped up the horses. They started off with a jolt. I'd been holding Celinda's hand through the window. I ran a bit, still holding her hand as the stage started off. Then I could no longer keep up. "Good-bye, Celinda, good-bye!"

In a moment or two I stood alone in the road watching the stage, a speck, disappearing into the blue hills of the Connecticut morning, silence all around me except for the chirping of the birds and the distant lowing of a cow.

All alone inside a stagecoach, I thought. Except for her lie. Well, I hope it serves her well. I do.

Chapter Three

O ctober went on. The nights became chilled and quilts were taken out. Warm colorful cloaks appeared on the backs of the Hannahs, Phoebes, and Amys. My father brought wood with his next load of vegetables. Fires appeared with regularity in all the hearths in all of the rooms. Lessons at the seminary had gone on through the summer months, but now it got more serious.

Sarah had started school in the middle of September; and by the second week of October the Board of Visitors knew about it. They did not come 'round themselves, of course. They sent their militia, the local matrons who appeared at the dark green front door. They said, in innocence, that they had come for tea.

Now, everybody who lives in New England knows that tea has not been an innocent occupation since the colonists threw it into Boston Harbor. But Miss Crandall said, "Oh, yes, of course, how could I have forgotten? Come in!"

"Is there something on your minds?" Miss Crandall asked as the tea progressed. I was helping Mariah serve it. Miss

Crandall is not one to mince words. "You look like a delegation," she said.

As everybody who lives anywhere knows, a delegation is the worst thing that can ever make its way into your home.

"We don't like it," said Mrs. Peters, wife of the Episcopal minister, "that a nigra girl is attending this school. We wish you to remove her. We will not have our daughters in such an establishment."

Apparently they were not about to mince words either.

"We want the girl of color out of the classroom," said Mrs. Daniel Frost. Her husband was the founder of the Canterbury Temperance Society. The others agreed.

Miss Crandall said no. Cups were clanked immediately down in saucers, mouths patted with linen napkins, looks exchanged, and the delegation of matrons stood and took their leave.

The third week in October came a letter from Mr. Importance himself, Miss Crandall's older brother, Mr. Hezekiah. He could not countenance this, he said. His wife was having her fifth child and he was worried that their business at his cotton mill on Mudhole Road would fall off if his sister disgraced the family in this way.

Now, I know how older brothers can be. I have Charles. Enough said. But I think Mr. Hezekiah was more worried about his uppity wife's family. She's a Cornell, and they are one of the oldest families in Canterbury.

Then came a letter from Mr. Reuben, Miss Crandall's

younger brother. He's a doctor, educated at Yale, and the one who wrote how Miss Crandall should remember how she was baptized. He hoped she would always be discreet, he wrote. And not disgrace them.

"Dear Reuben," Miss Crandall said as she read the letter to us, "he is such a darling." But I saw the tears in her eyes and wondered exactly how darling he was.

Next came Miss Crandall's father, who had the unlikely name of Pardon. Oh, he is as benign as his name, but there are times I fear him a bit daft. For instance, he cannot stand "gathered in" things. This means he cannot abide worldly possessions, or anything that detracts from his peace of mind. He will come around to the academy and fix anything that is broken, but he will not be about the place when it is time for spring or fall cleaning. To him, that is a "gathered in" event.

He told Miss Crandall that people had been coming to him and asking him to beg his daughter to come to her senses.

"What would thee have me do?" Miss Crandall asked him. She uses the Quaker "thee" and "thou" when speaking to her family. And they use it with her.

"Whatever thy heart dictates, daughter," he said.

Now, I can just hear my father saying such to me. But never mind. Miss Crandall had no intention of coming to her senses. She had found out how wonderful life could be if you got out of your senses once in a while. And what made this all so wonderful was that she was only putting her Quaker beliefs into action.

"'Do not fight with those who are wrong,'" she told us, "'but come to the aid of those who are oppressed.' That is the Quaker saying."

The thing about Quakers is they will not go to war, they say they will not fight, but when they decide to go to the aid of the oppressed, they fight with all the vengeance of St. Michael and his archangels.

Yet somehow I thought that Miss Crandall still did not know what would come of all this.

The fourth week in October came Miss Almira, Miss Crandall's younger sister. She was only seventeen to Miss Crandall's ancient thirty. I found myself staring at her. She was so pretty, her limbs so long, her face so pert, that she looked ready to burst out of her Quaker clothes. "Reuben sent me," she told Miss Crandall. "He wishes me to be a help to thee. He knows times are trying."

It was as if Miss Crandall immediately knew what this meant. "If Reuben sent thee to spy on me, to see that his interests are taken care of, to turn my girls against me, thee may leave now," she said.

"Why, sister, how can thee speak so? I am here to help." But the blue eyes twinkled mischievously.

Miss Crandall sighed. "Come in, then." I could see that she and Miss Almira did not get on, that she did not trust her sister. Or was it that her sister, so lovely and young, was an affront to her? That she reminded her of opportunities lost? I had heard that Miss Almira had many beaus. And there were none in sight, far as I could see, courting Miss Crandall.

The fourth week of October also came the Board of Visitors. Men in dark gray or black frock coats. And dark gray or black eyes. Men with hands either long and slim or fat and stubby that had never held a hoe or milked a cow. Men with high collars and silk cravats that they wore so tight if any goodness was in their hearts it was held therein and never allowed out.

Mr. Daniel Frost, Mr. Andrew T. Judson the lawyer. Dr. Andrew Harris, Mr. Rufus Adams, Justice of the Peace; Samuel Hough, who manufactured axes; Mr. William Kinne, secretary of the Congregational Church; and the minister of that church, the Reverend Dennis Platt; Captain Richard Fenner, and Solomon Paine.

They required much tea and cake. Mariah and I were so busy I could scarce pay mind to what was going on.

"We are perfectly willing that people of color be educated," said Mr. Judson, "provided it is done in some other town than Canterbury."

To this Miss Crandall replied: "Moses had a Negro wife."

They did not wish to discuss Moses. They wished to discuss Sarah. But this had silenced them for a moment.

"You consider yourselves part of Connecticut's revolutionary soil," Miss Crandall said. "I have heard you speak of it. What I am doing is following in the footsteps of our forefathers."

"I did not put up fifteen hundred dollars on the mortgage of this house to have you educate Negroes," said Mr. Hough, whose face looked at that moment remarkably like the axes he manufactured.

"Sarah Harris is my best pupil," Miss Crandall told them firmly. "This school may sink. But I will never give up Sarah!"

Dead silence followed. In unision the Board of Visitors stood up and set down their teacups. Mariah stood poised, pot in hand, ready to pour seconds. I stood behind her holding the tray with the sugar and cream. It was the shot heard 'round the world. Or at the very least, 'round Canterbury.

They reached for hats and filed out, one after the other, looking for all the world like a line of penguins that had decided they had come to the wrong island. The door closed behind them. Mariah and I stared at each other, then at Miss Crandall.

"Well," she sighed, "I've gone out on a limb now, haven't I? I might as well take the saw with me. Mary, fetch me pen and paper."

I ran. And I brought her book of addresses, too.

"I'll not need that, Mary," she said.

"But I know how you always forget Mr. Reuben's address," I said.

"Fetch me a copy of *The Liberator*," she directed. "The address I want is in there."

I near froze in my tracks, then bestirred myself.

"Oh, Mary." Her words stopped me at the door of the parlor.

"Yes, Miss Crandall?"

"Fetch it discreetly, will you, dear? No need to let anyone

else know I'm writing to Mr. Garrison. I can trust you to keep it a secret, can't I?"

"Oh, yes, ma'am. They could torture me and I'd never tell!"

She smiled. "I'm sure it won't come to that, Mary. Though it may come close."

Once in the next hour, I brought tea to the parlor for her. She was writing furiously, but looked up to thank me. "Come back soon," she said. "I shall want you to deliver this letter to the post office in time for the afternoon stage to Boston."

When I returned the letter was sealed and addressed boldly to "Mr. Lloyd Garrison, Editor, *The Liberator*, No. 11. Merchant's Hall, Congress and Water Streets, Boston, Massachusetts."

I stared at the delicately scrawled address on the cream-colored envelope as if it were addressed to the President himself. Then I felt Miss Crandall's hand on my arm.

"Don't be frightened, dear. If anyone in the world can help me now it is Mr. Garrison. I know he is flamboyant and oft times a troublemaker, but his words carry weight and travel far and wide. I may need that before I am through."

I left the house feeling as if I might just as well turn the letter over to the town crier, to the town criers of all of New England. I felt the weight of that letter, like a rock in my hands. And I recalled Sarah's words about Mr. Garrison. *He calls himself a peace-disturber, a fanatic, even a madman.*

Miss Crandall knew this. She read *The Liberator*. By the time I reached the post office I understood that Miss Crandall knew that if you wanted to deliver people from bondage and come to the aid of the oppressed, you must be willing to not only go out on a limb but take the saw with you. I also knew that when that limb went under the saw, we would all fall with her.

Chapter Four

━━━►◆◄━━━

D uring all this time things were not quiet at home. With so many children about in all phases of life, how could things be quiet? Four-year-old Jane Elizabeth got the croup. Eight-year-old Oliver brought a note home from school saying he was plaguing the teacher, and fourteen-year-old William pronounced that he wanted to leave school and work on the docks in Boston.

Mama and Daddy took this as the influence of Celinda's leaving. With all that was going on, they scarcely had time to miss her. But I caught Mama shedding quiet tears as she put away some of the things Celinda had left. And I know Mama and Daddy talked long on these autumn nights.

I also know they blamed themselves for Celinda's leaving. I had not told them she had put down on her paper that she was white. How did they think she'd gotten hired? Sometimes they befuddled me. Mayhap they knew more than they let on to us. Why, for instance, hadn't word of the commotion at the school reached them? If it had, why didn't they say something?

They didn't. Sarah said Daddy's desire for us to be educated washed away all other worries in his mind. She also warned me not to speak of the troubles at school. Sarah could read Daddy like a navigator at sea read the stars. She was the only one in the family who could get around him, and I had always depended upon her warnings.

The last week in October we received a letter from Celinda. She wrote that she was in a boardinghouse. The food was middling, but plentiful, the beds clean. She went to church of a Sunday. She was learning how to use the looms. Of course, it was hard work and her hands were already raw and her feet swollen. But soon she would be paid and send some money home.

This pronouncement brought tears to Daddy's eyes. He had not counted on having to accept money from a daughter who earned it by the sweat of her brow.

Then we had a visit at home, too. It was from Mr. Begley, a member of the American Colonization Society. The American Colonization Society was concerned with solving the "Negro problem." Their position was that it had been a mournful error to bring people of color into this country in the first place. And now they wanted to rectify that mistake by returning Negroes to a colony on the west coast of Africa called Liberia. Especially those who were not docile.

The Society had failed in the South, where they knew what to do with Negroes who were not docile. In the North they persisted in telling us that in Liberia we could prosper with our own kind. Mr. Begley had visited us before to try to talk

Daddy into taking his family to Liberia. Somehow we always knew he kept track of the free Negroes in Windham County.

"Two girls in your family are missing," he said as he sipped the tea I had served him in the parlor.

"Jane Elizabeth has the croup," Daddy told him, "and Celinda has gone off to work in Boston in the home of a genteel family."

I had never heard Daddy lie. None of us had.

Mr. Begley smiled. "Come now, Mr. Harris. I have my sources. I know your daughter Celinda went to work in the mills in Lowell."

A hush came over the room. "My daughter," Daddy said quietly, "is with a genteel family in Boston. I can give you a name if you wish."

I held my breath. I knew Daddy had friends in Boston. But had he gone this far to cover Celinda's tracks?

"That will not be necessary," Mr. Begley countered. "I shall not expose Celinda's place in the mills. I would not want to at any rate. Unless you force me to."

Daddy never wavered in his calmness. And he did not ask what Mr. Begley wanted from him. He just waited. Because he knew something was wanted.

"You see, I need a favor from you, Mr. Harris. That is, the Society needs a favor. We know where Celinda is. It is our business to know such things. We have a heartfelt interest in the futures of free people of color." He paused to sip some tea. "We would like you to let us bandy it about that your Celinda has gone to Liberia under the protection of the Society. It would cast a favorable light on our work and give encouragement for other young girls to do so."

Nobody spoke. Mr. Begley sipped more tea. "We would like you to let us publish this in our newspaper, *The African Repository*. It is the official newspaper of our Society."

"I know what it is," Daddy said crisply.

"We will give her a nice write-up. Make you proud. Wouldn't you rather, after all, have people think your daughter had gone back to live with her people, than that she passed herself as white, violating the laws, to work in the mills?"

"Her people are here. In Canterbury" was all Daddy would say.

It was a terrible moment for everybody. A moment in which every fear we had ever had was loosed. And every threat given free rein. I saw Sarah about to speak, saw Mama put her hand on Sarah's arm. I feared my sister would start in with her ravings and cause the end of Celinda's job at the mill. Or cause some other trouble to be brought down upon us.

Daddy got up and walked across the room. He looked out the window. Then he spoke. "This is America, Mr. Begley," he said. "You have a right to print in your newspaper whatever you wish. I am given to understand that is one of our freedoms."

"You will not dispute it, then?"

"If I had the time to dispute all the lies I read in newspapers, even *The Liberator*, I would have to neglect my work and let my family starve," Daddy said.

"Thank you, Mr. Harris. I will take my leave now."

Daddy did not turn around to bid him good-bye. And when he did turn around, I saw why. There were tears in his eyes. He had, by not protesting, allowed Celinda to keep her place at the mills. But he had also violated one of his most precious beliefs. No, two. First that you should never let anybody threaten you to do anything. And second, that you should not go against your principles to make a gain.

I wondered how long it would take before Mr. Begley found out that Sarah was a regular student at the seminary. Not long, once Mr. Garrison responded to Miss Crandall's letter.

Later in the dark of our room, Sarah whispered to me, "You see now why I have to do what I am doing, Mary? Do you see? They hold the power over us. We have got to break that power. Mr. Begley allowed Celinda to stay in the mill. But only if Daddy did his bidding."

"It near killed him," I said.

"There's something you don't know about our daddy, Mary. He'll do anything not to cause trouble. He wants only a peaceful life and his children educated. And he'll pay any price for it. He'll never take a stand for our race."

"That isn't true," I protested.

"No? Well why do you think he hates Charles being agent for *The Liberator*? Because *The Liberator* is a troublemaker newspaper. Believe this or not. But when your turn comes to make a stand of any kind for our race, don't tell him. Or you'll never get to do it."

I shuddered. What would he do when he found out Miss Crandall had asked help from *The Liberator*? What would he do when his desire for a peaceful life conflicted with his desire to have his children educated?

"What do you think Mr. Begley will do if he finds out we're both learning at the seminary?" I asked Sarah.

"Likely he already knows. Not much that man doesn't know."

"Then why didn't he say something tonight?"

"Do you tell all you know?" she flung at me.

I didn't answer.

"Nobody with any sense does. Anyways, the Colonization Society won't get in a tizzy over us learning. It's troublesome colored folk they concern themselves with. Like Celinda. Going to work in the mill. That's troublesome."

I fell asleep wondering how Celinda's troublesome was worse than Sarah's and mine. And how the Society decided such things.

Chapter Five

Christmas in New England, especially amongst Congregationalists, is not held in very high esteem. With Quakers it has even less. It has been deemed almost "papist" and there is nothing one can be hereabouts that is worse than papist. We had the usual church services and a cook made a special dinner. It was for the Hannahs, Phoebes, and Amys. Some even received packages from home.

Miss Crandall kept checking the mail. Everyone thought she too was expecting a Christmas package. But I knew she was waiting for an answer to her letter to Mr. Lloyd Garrison.

In January that letter came.

Miss Crandall could scarce conceal her excitement. But she made certain that Miss Almira did not see it. Or Mariah or Sarah. Since I was in her room when she opened it she simply said, "It's come, Sarah." And she smiled at me and put her finger in front of her lips for silence.

Soon after the letter arrived she gathered all her helpers

around her. "I must go to Boston," she said. "I wish to inquire about infant schools."

Everyone murmured. Infant schools? Was she going to expand, then, and take in infants?

She hushed them. "It depends on what I find," she said. And she smiled at me. "Mary, do you suppose if I wrote a note to your father he would allow you to accompany me?"

My heart beat a little faster. She was going to see Mr. Garrison! And taking me with her!

"Oh, Miss Crandall," Sarah whined. "I should be the one to accompany you!"

Miss Crandall smiled. "I need you here, Sarah, to help keep things going." And so she started writing to my father. I stood beside her, wondering if I should speak. Then I did. "Miss Crandall, I don't think my daddy would like it if he knew we were going to see Mr. Garrison," I said tremulously. "He doesn't even like copies of *The Liberator* in the house."

"Then I shall tell him I am going to look at infant schools. It isn't time yet to tell anyone the true purpose of our visit."

Before we left I paid a visit to Stephen's store. The day was gray and carried a chill that benumbed not only my body but my spirit. And when I approached the store I saw the CLOSED sign on the door. Closed in the middle of the day? Was something wrong? Then I saw a light behind the drawn shutters and decided to knock on the door anyway.

A shutter was pulled aside and when he saw me, Stephen

held up a finger as if to bade me wait. I waited, stamping my feet in the bone-chilling cold. Overhead the leaden skies promised snow. It was a day to be home by a fire, sewing or reading a book. The street was near deserted.

Finally, the front door of the store opened. Stephen stuck his head out, looked quickly up and down the street, and gestured for me to come inside.

"What are you about?" I asked. "You look pursued."

"Do I? Come in. Warm yourself. I've been taking stock for the New Year. I hate the job. Sit down, get warm. Can I offer you some tea?"

At that moment there came a thumping from under the wooden floorboards. "What's that?" I asked.

Stephen scowled. "Creatures. I think I've got some raccoons or possum under the floor. Must have made a home under there for the winter. I'll have to rout them out."

Why did I not believe him? "I thought you had a cellar below."

"There's a root cellar, of course. Can I get you some supplies today, Mary? Or is this just a visit?"

He was trying to distract me. "Both," I said. "We need some coffee beans. Used ours all up over Christmas. And I wanted to tell you that I'm going to Boston with Miss Crandall."

"Boston, is it? I envy you." He was measuring out the beans. "My uncle is in Boston."

"I know."

"I was supposed to visit him for Christmas, but I couldn't

leave the store. You're lucky. What's the reason for your visit?"

"Miss Crandall is going to look at infant schools," I lied. I wanted to tell him the truth, but could not violate Miss Crandall's trust in me. "I also wanted to tell you that a man came 'round from the Colonization Society to see Daddy. He knows Celinda's gone to the mills. He says the Society knows it, too."

He stopped measuring. "I've told no one, Mary."

"I know. And he promised to tell no one if Daddy let him bandy it about that she's gone to Liberia. He says it will encourage other young girls to do so."

Stephen secured a string around the sack of beans. "What'd your daddy do?"

"He went along with it. To protect Celinda."

He nodded, scowling. He looked so much older when he scowled. He brought the sack of beans over to me and dropped it in my basket. "Sometimes we have to lie to protect our own interests these days," he said. "I hate it, but people who pry deserve lies."

He looked at me as if I should take some meaning from this. I nodded. What was he trying to say? He was fetching something from behind the counter, a small bundle. He handed it to me. It was a fine linen handkerchief wrapped around some maple sugar candy and peppermints. "For you, for Christmas."

"Why, thank you, Stephen."

Just then there was more thumping under the floorboards.

"Darned creatures. I'll have to tend to them. Well, Mary, have a good trip. Don't forget to visit the bookstores. There's lots of fine bookstores in Boston." He was striding toward the door, to open it for me.

He wanted me to leave. Something was going on and he needed me out of there. I just knew it. But what? I smiled, thanked him again for the gift, and bade him good-bye. He locked the door and pulled the shutters closed behind me.

The trip in the stage to Boston was cold but exciting. We wrapped ourselves in rugs, and Miss Crandall had given me a new warm cloak, which was soft and almost elegant. It was of a lovely blue color. Because she was a Quaker she did not expect those around her to dress plain. My sister Sarah was envious of the cloak, I could tell. "I should be going, not you," she said. "I am the one sacrificing myself to attend this school. I am the object of hatred."

I felt Sarah's envy like a cold knife. Yet I was determined not to let it detract from my joy at this trip. All the way in the stage I tried to imagine what Boston would be like. But nothing I had ever known could prepare me.

We arrived around dusk, so the lights themselves seemed like magic to me. We saw some gaslight, but most impressive were the people huddled about in the city, people who were selling things and buying things. We passed a great building with many people milling about. Miss Crandall said it was very historic. She called it Faneuil Hall. We passed a place she called Dock Square. It was surrounded by business establishments. We went by a bustling market. There, merchants huddled around fires of pitch or coals. Smells also abounded, of sweet wood smoke, burning pitch, fish, horse droppings, coffee, fresh goods from bakeries.

"Fresh cod, haddock, and mackerel!" came the shouts. "Just in this day!"

There was the buzz of voices, the clopping of horses' hooves on the cobblestones, church bells. Looking across Dock Square, Miss Crandall pointed out a tall, narrow structure. "There," she said, "is the Charlestown battleground. There across the river."

"I want to stop," I told her. "I want to see all these places."

But she said no. So we went on, past stands piled high with vegetables. Oh, I thought, Daddy should see this. Past glass-windowed shops with fancy signs outside that said STATIONER and BOOKSELLER and PRINTING. Oh, I wanted to see these wondrous things. I wanted to be able to tell Sarah. And Stephen.

As we drove by a brick edifice with large numbers listed outside, Miss Crandall pointed. "There. Number 11. There is the office of *The Liberator*. But still we went on. "Why do you not stop?" I asked.

"I must invite him to meet me in our hotel dining room."

Mr. Barker's Hotel was the kind of an establishment that befitted a Quaker lady in her somber gray dress with the snow-white collar and her hair drawn back tightly in a bun. Along with her "helper," as she described me, in best wool dress, bonnet, and new cloak. The minute we settled in our rooms, Miss Crandall penned a note.

"The lady who wrote you a short time since would inform you that she is now in town, and should be very thankful if you would call at Mr. Barker's Hotel and see her a few moments this evening at six o'clock."

I nodded my solemn approval.

"I want to thank you for your trustworthiness, Mary," she said.

"I am honored to be included, ma'am," I said. "But I think you are going through an awful lot of trouble for my sister Sarah."

She raised her eyebrows. "This is not only for your sister Sarah, child. I realize I have not told you the real reason for our visit. I shall tell you now. In my original letter to Mr. Garrison I asked his advice respecting changing white scholars for colored ones."

I could not believe my ears. "You are going to allow misses of color in your school?"

"Yes."

Blood pounded in my head. "You are going to put the white girls out?"

"I have studied on it a long time, Mary. You see, what has happened with your sister has quickened me to action. I know now what my real purpose is. And with Mr. Garrison's help I shall then ask him for names of at least two dozen young women of good families from Boston and other cities near the seaboard."

I had to sit down. Weakness overcame me. The cheek of it! She was going to put out the Phoebes and Hannahs and Amys and let girls of color take their places! We are in trouble now, I told myself. How can she be so becalmed about it?

A terrible fear had swept into my heart, like a great black bird. I could feel the flapping of its wings inside my chest. Was this woman mad then? Or courageous?

I am not courageous, I thought. And then I thought, wait until Sarah finds out about this. She will think she started it all. Did she? Well she can take all the glory if she wants. I want no part of it. And then I told myself that it was too late. That I was part of it. And I did not have the mettle for it. And it was not fair for Miss Crandall to drag me into it without telling me first.

She was saying something. What? That we had only an hour before supper.

When we were seated in the elegant dining room of the hotel awaiting Mr. Garrison, I busied myself looking out onto the street, into the darkness, watching the carriages and people pass by. I pushed all thoughts of Miss Crandall's plans from my head. At home in such darkness everyone would be off the streets. Here street lamps lit the night and life went on.

"How will we know Mr. Garrison?" I asked.

"He will know us. Not many Quaker ladies will be waiting for him."

Not many Quaker ladies are crazy enough, I thought. At that moment I saw a man come into the dining room holding his hat in his hand and looking around. He was dressed all in black with a wide linen collar over the neck of his frock coat. His jaw was long and square and he had a dimple in his chin which seemed at odds with the solemn face. He was tall and thin and had lost most of the hair on his head. He wore spectacles.

There were no cloven feet. There was no eye patch. He looked more like a poet than an upstart newspaperman. Yet, as he cast his eyes around the room, I sensed something of the besieged about him, like a hare pursued by a fox. His smile, when he sighted us, lit up his face and he crossed the room in a few strides to bow over Miss Crandall, who offered her hand.

He kissed it. "Miss Crandall," he said, "we have something in common."

"And what is that?" Miss Crandall asked.

"I have received many letters from the South complaining of the malign influence of Quakers, itinerants, and fanatical Yankee editors."

"Oh? And do you consider yourself fanatical, then, Mr. Garrison?"

"I aspire to it," he said.

He sat down. She introduced me. He smiled. "I love children," he said. "My one disappointment in life is that I have not yet had time to wed and become a father."

The waiter came and they ordered dinner, fish and potatoes and something green. She asked him more about the letters from the South and he said that what hurt more than the complaints was the postage due on the letters.

They laughed. "One letter," he said, "came from Nelly Custis Lewis, granddaughter of Martha Washington. She wrote that I merit the death penalty for making innocent Southerner slave holders feel as if they are sitting on a smothered volcano."

"You have done wonderful work," Miss Crandall told him. "I come late to your way of thinking. But now that I come to it, I would ask your advice."

"Keep the little miss of color at your school," he said. "The more mischief we make for the unrighteous, the more it aids our cause."

"Mr. Garrison," Miss Crandall said, "I intend to make more than mischief. Do not underestimate me because I am a woman."

That brought him up short. His fork paused midair. "Dear lady, I apologize if I give such an impression," he said. "How can I help with what you intend to do?"

She told him. The long poet's face grew even more solemn. "You wish," he whispered, "to exchange all the daughters of the influential men at your school for misses of color?"

It seemed that the very candles on the table flickered when she told him yes, this is what she wished. He set down his fork. He sat back. He wiped his mouth with his napkin. He took a sip of water. "This is a transfiguring moment," he said, "even for me."

We waited and I determined to ask Miss Crandall later what transfiguring meant.

"I wish names of good Negro families whose daughters might become students," she said. "I wish you to run an ad in *The Liberator* announcing that I am accepting misses of color."

"All this I will gladly do for you, dear lady."

"And I wish, Mr. Garrison, not to be used by the abolitionists in their cause," she finished. "I wish to open my school and have it work without becoming a pawn of the abolitionists."

How could she say such to him? Was she being coy? Or outright lying?

"This last I cannot promise you," he said. "Once you do what you wish to do you will loose all kinds of demons. Once they are loosed, I cannot stop them."

She nodded. "As long as you do not aid them," she said.

Chapter Six

Whatever otherworldly vows were made between them that evening as the candles flickered on the table, I do not know. I was growing sleepy. The ride in the cold stage, the sights and sounds and smells of Boston, the rich food, all conspired to make me sleepy. I dimly remember Mr. Garrison saying he knew some people in Canterbury, that he had "connections" there. But to reveal their names would endanger them.

I believed him. This was a dangerous man, I decided. A man to be reckoned with. Yet a good man, I sensed that, too. Then it came to me. How can a man be both good and dangerous?

I was excused and took myself to bed while they were still conspiring. I fell asleep under a soft quilt with the sounds of carriages and people talking on the street below. When I woke a bright fire was in the hearth, sun poured in the windows, and breakfast had been delivered to the room. Miss Crandall sat reading.

"Hurry and eat," she said. "We must go to see the newspaper office of Mr. Garrison this day. And then we're going to visit a Negro family in Providence, Rhode Island."

I decided I had best forget about the bookstores. And my mouth watered as we passed three on the way to the office of *The Liberator*.

Mr. Garrison showed us around as if the place were the site of historic interest.

"This is my Ramage handpress. It is secondhand. So is the type." He gestured to cases of small black letters laid out on a sturdy oak table. "You must forgive the ink-stained windows and the dirty walls, Miss Crandall, but when it gets busy in here at night, no one notices the decay."

"Where do you live?" Miss Crandall asked. I saw her eyebrows go up at the disarray around her, and knew that her Quaker sensibilities were offended.

"Right here, dear lady. Me and my friend Mr. Knapp. We sleep on pallets, right here. Our needs are few. We live on bread and milk, a bit of fruit and some cake, which the people in the downstairs shops kindly give us."

"You are wanting," Miss Crandall said.

"The Lord provides," he told her. "And we sleep here not only to save money but to guard the presses. Now there is little time. I must soon be back. Let us be off."

"Remember," Miss Crandall said as she put her hand on my arm in the stage. "Remember, dear Mary. You have been inside the office of *The Liberator*. You have met the man who is devoting his life to freeing your people. You will be able to tell your grandchildren of it someday."

We went to Providence, to the boarding house of Elizabeth Hammond. It was in a neighborhood tumbling down, a neighborhood where refuse was in the streets, where white sailors lounged outside rowdy saloons. Miss Crandall said it was a place of much crime, where violence of white folk against Negroes often happened.

Elizabeth Hammond was a widow, Miss Crandall explained. She had two daughters, Ann Eliza, who was seventeen, and Sarah, who was nine. The girls were not at home but in a local school. On this cold day we found Elizabeth Hammond on her knees in the dining room of her boardinghouse, scrubbing the floors. The water in the pail steamed.

"I try and try," she said, as she stood to greet us, "to keep the influence of the streets out."

The floor shone, as if she had scrubbed the stuff of her nightmares away.

She was a tall thin woman with a turban on her head and eyes that had a yellow light in them. Her voice was soft, her diction perfect.

"I am pleased to meet you," said Miss Crandall.

"The pleasure is mine. Mr. Garrison here sent around a note that you would like to educate my girls."

"Yes. And others of good families. If you can refer some to me."

"Do you have a pen of gold, Miss Crandall? And a stone tablet, perhaps?"

"I beg your pardon?"

Elizabeth Hammond smiled. "You cannot have less, surely. For you are an angel sent by the Lord himself. Come, sit. Here at the table. I'll have Moria bring some hot coffee and cinnamon cake. Let me go and make myself presentable."

I peered around the dining room while she was gone. A white cloth covered the long table. The room was narrow and dark. How different, I thought, from the dining room at the school, with its large windows and organdy curtains.

Moria came with the coffee and cake. She was young, as young as I, surely, and at first she just stood there in the doorway with her tray, staring at Mr. Garrison.

"Come in, child," Miss Crandall said. "Did you make the cake yourself?"

The girl did not answer. She circled wide of Mr. Garrison as she set the tray down. As one would circle the throne of the Lord Himself. Mr. Garrison smiled at her. She fled the room.

"She should be taught better manners," Miss Crandall said.

"She is in awe of Mr. Garrison," I offered.

"One should be in awe only of the Lord," Miss Crandall replied.

But I saw the pleased expression on Mr. Garrison's face.

When Elizabeth Hammond came to join us at the table, the

first thing she asked was about the cost of the school.

"The tuition is three dollars a term and a dollar and fifty cents a week for board. Their laundry will be done for them," Miss Crandall said. "But if you cannot afford it, Mrs. Hammond, we can find a way to take your girls anyway."

"I can afford the tuition, Miss Crandall. Why do you think I run this place? So when my girls they grow up they will not have to clean up the dirt of others. So they will not have to live in a neighborhood where there is a riot in the streets near every day."

Mr. Garrison nodded knowingly.

"But tell me something," Elizabeth Hammond said. "How will the white girls in your school receive my Ann Eliza and Sarah?"

"The white girls will no longer be there," Miss Crandall answered. "I intend to ask their parents to take them all out and replace them with girls of color."

Mrs. Hammond was taken aback. She seemed to grasp the importance of the matter even more than I. "And are these white girls who are there now of eminence?"

"Hannah Pearl is the daughter of a state senator. Others have similar backgrounds. And some are the daughters of squires or wealthy farmers."

"And where will these girls go if you turn them out?"

"They will have to go abroad for an equal education."

"Then you will incur the wrath of your town folk, Miss Crandall."

"I know that. I am willing to risk it."

Mrs. Hammond pondered the matter. "Will my girls be safe in Canterbury?"

"Far safer than they are here, Mrs. Hammond. I promise you."

"You will be helping to bring down the great bastille of slavery, Mrs. Hammond," Mr. Garrison told her.

"All I want," she said looking at him, "is a good education for my daughters. What bastilles fall in the process does not interest me."

Of a sudden I sensed matters at play here that were at odds. Mr. Garrison kept talking about slavery, Miss Crandall about desiring to find at least eighteen more young ladies of color for the school, and Elizabeth Hammond about what a wonderful opportunity this would be for her girls. Even I knew they were all speaking of different things. I wondered if they all knew it.

Chapter Seven

I could not wait to return home. At the same time I was frightened and dreaded it. I wished we could travel on forever, Miss Crandall and I, and never go home to finish what she was starting. Things changing all around me, getting ugly. I was no longer taken with the sights, sounds, and smells of Boston. I wanted my daddy's house, my mama's arms. I knew, without being told, that my world was becoming unraveled.

On our last morning in Boston as we were having our breakfast in the hotel a tall, stately young Negro made her way across the dining room to stand by our table.

"Miss Crandall, I am Ann Eliza Hammond," she said.

You would think she was Lucretia Mott, the Quaker feminist, the way Miss Crandall carried on. "Oh my dear, do sit down. I am so overjoyed to meet you!"

I did not like the girl on sight. Something there was about her, though I could not put a name to it. She did not look at me at all, only at Miss Crandall. Seventeen, I minded. She is only seventeen? Then how comes she to that look in her eye? And what does it bespeak?

"I am honored, Miss Crandall," she said, "to be one of your lambs. Though it means I go to slaughter. I have long wanted to do something for the cause. Oh, don't tell my mother that, please. All she wants is that I get an education. My mother is a wonderful woman, Miss Crandall, but clearly, she knows nothing of the oppressed."

Miss Crandall folded her hand over Ann Eliza's. "You are one of us," she said.

I supposed she was, though I did not know what the requirements were. And I was determined then and there that if Ann Eliza belonged to the circle, I did not want to be part of it. She sounded like a fanatic, I minded. And then I thought, Sarah will love her. And I felt ashamed. Did that mean, then, that Sarah was a fanatic?

It had been snowing since first light and there was already two inches on the ground when we boarded the morning stage. Ann Eliza and Mr. Garrison were both there. "I will come as soon as you send for me," Ann Eliza cried. "Send for me soon!"

Mr. Garrison shouted something about courage. I turned to look back as we drove away. And I could swear that in the spot where he'd stood there was a cloven hoofprint in the snow.

❄ ❄ ❄

We spent two days in New York City, a place without trees or grass or white fences, a place offensive to the eye as well as the other senses. We visited the houses of nine families. They all spoke the same way. They said things like: "We must stir the passions of the human heart." And: "We must act for our brothers and sisters who are still in chains."

They all knew Mr. Garrison. They all read his newspaper. And they all promised their children to Miss Crandall. By the time we boarded the packet boat home I saw her as I'd never seen her before. As a pied piper who had charmed the children out of these hardworking people. And by the time we arrived home I felt truly in the grip of a horrible howling destiny. True, I was tired, and it was freezing cold and late and dark, and behind the windows of all the houses whale oil lamps cast their light, yellow and welcoming and safe.

Why can't my life be like those of the inhabitants of those houses, I asked myself. Why must I be part of a cause?

The seminary was dark, as the stage pulled up in front and we disembarked. But no, there were two men on the front steps. One held a lantern. "Yes?" Miss Crandall asked, "may I help you gentlemen? Oh, Sheriff Coit, it's you. Is everything all right?"

She paid the driver and he set our portmanteaus down on the step and drove off. Sheriff Coit turned and the light from his lantern spilled out on the path. "This is Mr. Grimes from Savannah, Georgia," the sheriff said. And Mr. Grimes stepped out of the shadows and took off his hat. He was well dressed as became a gentleman of the day, but light from the lantern showed a puffy face with small, mean, greedy eyes. He shivered in the cold though he wore a cloak.

"Y'all sure do have some cold winters up heah," he said.

"How may I assist you, Mr. Grimes?" Miss Crandall asked. "It is cold. And late. My assistant and I have just returned from New York and are quite weary."

"This won't take but a minute, Miss Crandall," the sheriff said. "Mr. Grimes is an overseer on a plantation in Savannah. He comes seeking a mulatto slave who escaped by boarding a ship at the wharves. Some seamen hid him in bales of cotton being shipped north."

"Good for them," Miss Crandall said.

"Now, Miss Crandall," the sheriff admonished, "this slave is expensive property."

"No man is property," Miss Crandall said.

Overhead a night bird called. We stood in the circle of light from the sheriff's lantern, the four of us, and I knew Miss Crandall would stand here the night if need be and argue the sanctity of the human soul. We would freeze to death, surely.

"The vessel found berth in New York City," the sheriff went on. "And the slave connected with those who help his kind. Mr. Grimes was told by workers at the wharves that the man was directed to Connecticut. He was seen in Litchfield and New Haven, and some say here in Canterbury."

"He is not in my house, Mr. Grimes," Miss Crandall said. "I

can promise you that. But if he is not, it is only because my work as schoolmistress keeps me so busy that I have not yet had time to join the agency of brave souls here in the North who are helping people escape."

"There are such people then in Canterbury?" Mr. Grimes asked.

"If there are, Mr. Grimes, I do not know of them. And if I knew, I would not say. Now, as I said before, it is late. My assistant and I are weary from our travels and long for warmth and bed."

"The runaway goes by the name of Cato," Mr. Grimes said. He gave a little bow. "Thank you, ma'am." He wore polished boots and they crunched on the stones as he moved away.

"Help you with the baggage," Sheriff Coit offered, but Miss Crandall declined and we struggled with it ourselves, setting it in the front hall. Miss Crandall locked the door.

"It's so good to be home," she said. A lamp was burning. A tray of tea and buttered bread was on a table in the front parlor. The fire in the grate burned cheerfully. We sat and took tea in the silent house.

"Are there people in Canterbury who help runaway slaves?" I asked her.

"Yes."

"Do you know who they are?"

"I am not sure who they are."

"How do they help them?"

"You heard. They are smuggled, in wagons and on ships.

They are given clothing and food, directed to and hidden in certain houses on their way to safety. Often it is Canada."

"But how could anybody hide a runaway Negro here in Canterbury?" I asked. "Everybody knows everybody."

She sipped her tea. "They are hidden in barns, in attics, in cellars. Sometimes they sleep under floorboards until it is time for them to go."

The fire crackled then, sending out a spark. It landed on the Persian carpet. She stood and kicked it quickly onto the brick hearth, picked up a poker, and pushed some embers back.

I felt for a moment as if it had landed on me. I felt as if she was pushing around my brains with that poker. I felt the light, the heat.

I saw Stephen Coit's face, heard the thumping under his floor. And I knew then what name to give to the thumping.

Cato.

Who would have suspected it about mild Stephen Coit? And his father the sheriff, here this night to help find the fugitive.

I was glad Miss Crandall's back was to me. My face would give me away if she saw it just then. She went on fussing with the fire. "You must stay the night," she said. "There is a small room on the third floor. Very comfortable. Come, I will show you."

I followed her up the flights of stairs, our footsteps echoing the thumping of the runaway slave under Stephen Coit's floor. In my mind's eye all I saw was the face of that Southern overseer, puffy from excessive living, with those small, mean, greedy eyes. That night they haunted me. I saw them in my sleep.

Chapter Eight

In the next few days, it was difficult to keep my tongue still about what I had seen and what I knew, and of course I said nothing to anyone of what I surmised about Stephen Coit. When I woke the next morning in the small room on the third floor I reexamined the thought, as I minded the rag rugs on the wide floorboards, the cunning little window that gave such a bird's-eye view of the green outside, and the warm fire in the hearth.

The thought about Stephen held. He was harboring runaway slaves.

From downstairs came the noisy chatter of the Amys, Phoebes, and Hannahs at breakfast. How wonderful it would be, I thought, to sit in that sun-filled dining room, with the good china and the blue teapot from Holland on the table, and be waited on and have breakfast. How I envied them! At home now I would be serving the porridge out to the little ones, cleaning up their spills, rushing to help Mama stack the dishes before I came here, foregoing my own breakfast, and grabbing a piece of bread as I ran out the door.

I wondered. If Miss Crandall managed to bring girls of color into the school, would they be served like the white girls at table? Would I be included? I dressed and went down to the kitchen where I would put together the makings of my breakfast and mayhap help Mariah serve. I found Sarah already arrived from home, helping. She gave me a letter from Celinda.

"Well, did you have a wonderful time in Boston?" Her voice was tinged with envy.

"It was very interesting," I said.

"Did you visit the bookstores?"

"We didn't have time."

"How could you go to Boston and not visit a bookstore? Will you forever be a country bumpkin?"

I put Celinda's letter in my apron pocket. Then from the dining room I heard Miss Almira's voice. "Well, Prudence, did thee find out about infant schools?" There was an edge to it, much as Sarah's had.

"Yes, I visited a few," Miss Crandall replied. "But I'm afraid they're not for us."

"Come now, Prudence," her sister coaxed mischievously. "What did thee really do in Boston?"

"Do? Why, I have told thee, Almira. Does thee not believe me?"

Mariah smiled at me as the voices drifted into the kitchen.

"The whole place is out of sorts," she said.

I finished helping her, found a quiet corner, and read the letter from Celinda. She was doing well. Finally her feet weren't swollen anymore and she had, at long last, learned to thread the looms. A girl who worked two looms over had caught her dress in some machinery, been pulled in and near crippled. She'd had to go home. The foreman at the mill had forbidden more than one petticoat under their dresses. *And in the winter, she said, when it is so cold. But I suppose it is for the best, being the safest course to follow.*

Two girls in her dormitory had persistent coughs. *It's the cotton fibers that always seem to be present in the air,* she wrote. *It is said they get into the lungs. But not all the news is so doleful, sister. I have joined a literary society. It is a fine pastime when one works seventy-three hours a week. But after all, I am earning $3.25 a week and consider myself lucky. How would I earn this money at home? Room and board is only $1.25 a week and I have a whole $2 left over. Did I tell you that Daddy said I should bank my money, and not send any more home? He says he sent much of his fall harvest into the city this year. Only, please, he says, don't tell Sarah. You can keep a secret, I know. You must write soon.*

I put the letter down, feeling ashamed because Celinda was working so hard and not complaining. And because I had not been paying mind to what was going on at home. So Daddy had found a new market in the city. What city? Boston, most likely.

I tried to imagine myself at the looms. Or living in a crowded boardinghouse in a cold bedroom, having mush for breakfast and my feet swollen from standing on them constantly the first few weeks. I could not. I went to my chores and studies that day more diligently than ever.

At home it was difficult to keep what I knew to myself and not tell Mama and Daddy of Miss Crandall's plans. Or of what I suspected about Stephen Coit. I stayed away from his store. When Mama needed some supplies fetched, I sent sister Olive in my stead.

On my third day home Miss Crandall called me to her private room. "Mary," she said. "How would you like to live here?"

"Live here?" I looked at her dumbly.

"Yes, dear. I do enjoy your company. And in the next few weeks I will have need of your services even more than before." There was a light in her eyes that said more than her words.

"You could sleep in that little room on the third floor. Do you like it there? Is it warm enough? I could have a small desk brought there for you."

Oh, heaven! "I would most like it," I said. "If Mama and Daddy give permission. But what about Sarah?"

"I have no need for Sarah to board here yet. When the other girls come, she will stay."

So she was going ahead with her plans. "And are they coming, then?"

"I'm doing all I can to make it a reality, Mary. And you are the only one I can confide in. I'd love to confide in Almira. But somehow she seems too young, younger than you. I suppose because she's the baby of the family and we've all spoiled her so. And pretty." She sighed. "She has all these beaus, Mary. I suspect she'll be wed before she's twenty. My mother was wed at fifteen, you know."

"No, I didn't, ma'am."

"Yes, and now that nice John Rand seems of a mind to court Almira. I don't suppose I'll ever be courted, Mary. And as un-Quakerish as it is, I must confess I'm a bit jealous."

"I think you're prettier than Miss Almira, Miss Crandall."

She smiled. "Thank you, but that is vanity. We are all beautiful in the eyes of the Lord."

"Ma'am, can I ask you something?"

"Yes, of course, Mary."

"Have they found Cato yet?"

"Not that I have heard, Mary. Though I'm sure by now that he is already on his way to Canada."

"How does he get to Canada from here?"

"Why, there are several carefully planned routes on the freedom road," she said.

That was all she would say.

She wrote a note to Mama and Daddy asking if I could move into the school. They read the note, smiled, and said yes. Mama and Daddy trusted her. Mama helped pack my bags that evening. And that evening Daddy hitched up the wagon and drove me back to the seminary. But not before I faced down Sarah in the kitchen.

"You little sneak," she said, when Daddy was taking a box of my things out to the wagon and Mama was upstairs making sure I'd left nothing behind. "You've really ingratiated your-self with Miss Crandall, haven't you?"

I didn't even know what ingratiated meant. "It is her idea," I said.

"All the time being friends with me and working behind my back."

"I never!" Tears came to my eyes. Sarah and I quarreled sometimes, she bossed me around, but she was my older sister and I loved her. Her words were like a whip slashing at my soul. I could not abide being thought of by her like this.

She saw what she was doing to me, but kept on. "I can just imagine the sob story you gave her in Boston about having to do chores here at home."

"I never!"

"Bad-mouthed Mama and Daddy. Miss Fancy-Drawers can't live on a poor farm anymore."

"I don't think of this place as poor," I said.

"Then you don't know what's going on. They're living a meager existence here. And now you're abandoning them!"

"Sarah, don't talk such nonsense to your sister!" Daddy had come back inside the house and stood listening in the small vestibule just inside the door. "We are not living a meager existence! I will not have such talk from my children! And even if I were, I would never keep my children home to help if it meant not bettering themselves!"

"Sorry, Daddy." And Sarah ran upstairs.

And so I moved into Miss Crandall's seminary. She gave

me a fine quilt for my bed and a small desk and chair. I loved the small room on the third floor. It was like being in a snug bird's nest.

Within a week Miss Crandall called everyone together and made her announcement. In the keeping room the rain slashed against the windows, a cold freezing rain that set the mood. Candlelight flickered on the faces of the Amys, Hannahs, and Phoebes. Everyone knew some sort of announcement was coming, ever since our trip to Boston and New York.

Miss Almira's face was glowing. Mariah had told me that Miss Almira expected that her sister had met someone in New York, was about to become betrothed and step down as director and name her sister in her stead. And Miss Almira not yet twenty! And so flighty that so far Miss Crandall had used her mainly to run errands.

"Dear girls," Miss Crandall began. "I have arrived at my decision after much thought. I have had a regular wrestling with my conscience. As of the end of this week this school will be closed. I have written to all of your parents and they will come to fetch you home."

There was a general cry of dismay. There were some questions, some outbursts of "Why, why? Are you ill, Miss Crandall?"

Miss Crandall held up her hand for silence. "I am not ill. Nor am I betrothed, as some rumors have it." At this she cast a look at Miss Almira, who simpered and looked at the floor. "But my conscience has pricked me enough for me to take unusual action. I am opening this school to little misses of color. As of the first of April."

Now the silence was a shocked one. *Little misses of color?*

"Negro girls, you idiot," I heard one soft-spoken Amy whisper to one Hannah. "She's gone daft! Wait until my father finds out about this!"

"From where?" another whispered. "There aren't enough Negro girls in all New England to take our places."

"Take our places! That's just it!" from another. "She's putting us out! For Negroes!"

"Enough chatter!" Miss Crandall had heard some of it. So had my sister Sarah, who didn't know whether to look pleased or horrified. Miss Crandall's sister knew how to look, though. And what to say. She grabbed Miss Crandall's arm.

"Thee can't," she said. "Thee will be ruined!"

"To be ruined in the cause of righteousness is a blessing, sister."

"We'll all be ruined! Thee will bring the wrath of the town down upon us!" Miss Almira wailed. She who looked as if she never knew what righteousness was all about. Likely she was thinking of Mr. Reuben's wrath. Hadn't Miss Crandall said he had sent her to spy?

All this was spoken in frantic whispers, but luckily the students, involved in their own frantic whispers, did not hear this exchange.

"Ruined for following my conscience, sister? Hasn't thee forgotten our upbringing?"

Miss Almira stamped her foot, scowled, and turned away. Miss Crandall restored order. Some of the Amys, Phoebes, and Hannahs were crying, others bemoaning the loss of their friends. Miss Crandall went amongst them, soothing and placating.

Sarah pulled me from the room. "You knew this! You knew it all the time!"

What could I say? I stood there in the back hall watching the rain pouring down the windows. "Why do you blame me?" I asked. "You started it by asking to come here. You gave her the idea. Did you think you should be the only girl of color allowed?"

Sarah's lips were trembling. She wanted to kill me and, all at the same time, the wonderfulness of what was about to happen was falling over her, like a blanket against the freezing rain. She looked to the bleak light in the window as if it were the burning bush revealed to Moses. "I was the first one," she said. "And I did give her the idea. Remember how she said that the school might sink but she would never give up Sarah?"

"How could I ever forget it?"

Of a sudden she hugged me. I felt her heart beating in her breast. And I knew that the hug had nothing to do with me, or her loving me, at all.

After supper Miss Crandall had the girls all write letters home, saying they would be well looked after until their parents arrived. A desolation settled over the house that seemed to creep into the very corners, like mold. School officially closed on Friday, but for the next few days the girls could not be coaxed into study. So Miss Crandall left them to their own devices. They packed. They exchanged addresses, they huddled in each other's rooms.

By Friday the carriages started pulling up in the front round-about and solemn, grim fathers came to the door to fetch their daughters' portmanteaus, to mumble a few words, and to be off. As if the place was quarantined.

In one or two instances ominous but veiled threats were spoken by these fathers, dire warnings given. Miss Crandall responded in her usual cheerful manner, wishing them all well.

One after another the carriages came and left. Then, of a sudden the house was quiet and the rooms echoed. The books and globes and scientific equipment lay about.

"Abandoned," said Miss Almira. I was helping her straighten a classroom.

"Waiting," said Miss Crandall who came by the door just then. "Waiting."

"For what?" Miss Almira asked. "What will I do now?"

"Thee will help me with the new students," Miss Crandall said.

Miss Almira looked aghast.

"Does thee not wish to follow the Quaker teachings?" Miss Crandall asked. "To come to the aid of the oppressed?"

Miss Almira walked out of the room and did not answer at all.

Chapter Nine

Once again came the Board of Visitors. The very next morning as I dressed for breakfast in the quiet house I heard men's voice from belowstairs. More fathers, I thought. Come back, likely to persuade Miss Crandall to change her mind and take back their daughters. Or mayhap to threaten her.

I crept down the stairs. I could see the men in the front parlor. They were all dressed in black and sported canes. They wore high, stiff collars. Mariah was serving tea and fresh cinnamon. Words were flying like swords. You could hear their crashing.

"I will not retract and add to the mountain load of insults and injuries already heaped on the people of color in this country!" From Miss Crandall.

"You are changing the natural order of things!" From Mr. Daniel Frost, who looked every bit of what his name implied.

"You betray your community!" From Dr. Andrew Harris.

"And where will these Negro girls worship? At our

Congregational Church! Think of the embarrassment to them!" From Mr. Rufus Adams.

"You are inviting mongrelization! First you educate them, next they will be wanting to marry white men!" From Mr. Richard Fenner.

I stood in the hall, along with Mariah. I shivered. Outside, the February wind rattled the windowpanes. Inside, the rattling was far worse. Then came the most ominous threat of all.

"We shall have a town meeting!"

Two weeks later I was home for a visit to catch up with my family before the new girls came. I sat across from Daddy at our kitchen table at home. Overhead a whale oil lamp cast shadows of doubt across his face. "Why must I go back?" I asked. "Why can't I stay here with you and Mama? You need me. Olive can't do all the chores."

"What chores are there in the middle of winter that we can't do, child?" he asked.

I had no reply for this.

"You have an agreement with Miss Crandall," Daddy said. "She invited you into her home. She offered to educate you. Do you know what a gift that is?" His voice fair shook with depth of feeling.

"I don't like it there anymore, Daddy. The house is so empty. Miss Almira and Miss Prudence argue all the time. I never knew Quakers argued so. Sarah walks about like the queen of Sheba and gets special treatment, and all the while she tells me that things are going to get even more dolorous than they are now. She says the Board of Visitors will ride Miss Prudence out on a rail. And us with her."

"The fuss will die down," he said. "All you need be concerned with is your studies."

"Daddy, you don't understand," I said.

"And what is it that I do not understand, daughter? Tell me, then?"

"They are going to have a town meeting."

He nodded solemnly. "This is what these people do when they are threatened, daughter."

"Miss Crandall has written for help of friends. No one has come." I did not tell that she had written to Mr. Garrison for help. Mayhap I should have.

"When is the meeting?"

"Next week."

"They will come. These abolitionists stick together. It would not be good for her cause to have her represent herself at the meeting."

I couldn't not tell the rest, though. "Mr. Garrison wrote about her in *The Liberator*."

He nodded. "I saw the article. I read that paper."

"It was so terrible, Daddy! Even Miss Crandall said such. He made her sound like someone else! He made the school sound like someplace I never heard of! She said he vilified the people in town who oppose her school and it was not what she wanted."

"This man uses words like musket balls," Daddy said. "It is his way."

"And there's more, Daddy. I haven't told it all yet."

"Then tell me daughter, by all means."

"Mr. Hezekiah came today. He shouted so the walls shook. Then he said that tomorrow I must appear before him and recite what I have learned so far at the school."

"And so you will," he said. "And you will do your learning justice. And your teacher proud."

"He said, 'This child is a perfect example. If she performs well and justifies the experiment I might be inclined to change my mind.'"

"Then you will perform well, certainly."

"Daddy, it isn't fair to put me under such an obligation."

"Well then, what did Miss Crandall say?"

"First she had to quiet Miss Almira and Sarah. Both said my learning wasn't sufficient to make Mr. Hezekiah see things clearly. Sarah wanted to stand in my stead. But Miss Crandall said no, I was exactly the person Mr. Hezekiah needed to hear recite, a child whose mind could be formed. They spoke about me like I wasn't there. I felt like a piece of chattel."

"You must show them what you have learned, daughter. Do us proud."

"I feel as if it has nothing to do with me or my learning anymore."

"Yes it has. Don't lose heart. Let these white people fight amongst themselves. Like I said, it will die out. Would you rather be back at the district school? How would you fit in there now after what you have been exposed to?"

"The seminary isn't a nice place anymore, Daddy." I was losing the argument.

"The world is not a nice place, child. I thought we prepared you for that."

He looked so sad. If only I could tell him, I thought, what really worries me. How Sarah was growing more strange by the day, telling me that when the town meeting was over they would come and take all the colored girls who were in the school and throw us in jail. "And I will be the first!" she boasted. "I will go to jail like Joan of Arc! And afterward everyone will know my name. And I shall make speeches, like Lucretia Mott. And become famous."

If only I could tell him how Miss Crandall had cried at reading the newspaper article by Mr. Garrison, and said, "What have I done? I never meant for all this to be."

"Is there anything else, daughter?" Daddy asked.

"No, Daddy."

"Then you get a good night's sleep. And tomorrow I will deliver you bright and early back to school. And you will show Mr. Hezekiah what you have learned. And he will stop his shouting."

"Do you think we could stop at Stephen Coit's store first?"

"So early in the morning?"

"Yes. I'd like to bring Miss Crandall some fresh coffee beans."

"A good thought, daughter. A present. I shall give you money. I'm glad you are thinking clearly."

He had another customer, Mr. Hough, a lawyer. His daughter Phoebe had been one of the girls at the school. Mr. Hough was buying a pair of leather gloves. "Lost my others," he told Stephen. "When I moved my daughter out of that school." He looked up, saw me, and paid me no mind. "Can you ponder the curious turn that Miss Crandall has taken? Turning out white girls of leading families to open her school to Negroes?"

"She's a brave lady," Stephen said.

"Brave!" Mr. Hough slapped his money down on the counter and took his gloves. "I'd say addled is more the word for what she is." And he stomped out, glowering at me as he went.

Stephen smiled. "What can I do for you, Mary?"

"I'd like some coffee beans. A pound of your best, please. They're for Miss Crandall."

He measured out the beans. "Word is all over town about the school. She's got everybody in a dither, all right."

"Did you find the creature under your floorboards?"

For a moment he was puzzled, then he smiled. "Oh yes. It was a raccoon, as I thought. Pesky critters, always foraging about for food."

"Did you kill him?"

"No, of course not. I sent him on his way." He smiled at me

and I saw the lie in his eyes. And the truth. "Good luck at school now. Study hard and give Miss Crandall my best. Oh yes, here, I can't let you go off without a goodly supply of candy." He prepared another small bundle.

"Thank you, Stephen." I felt a glow of warmth between us. Then as I started out the door he called out to me.

"And you tell Miss Crandall if she's ever in need of any-thing to call on me. You hear?"

I heard him loud and clear as I went out the door.

Chapter Ten

━━◆━━

Surely nature had done everything in her power to render Mr. Hezekiah Crandall unpleasant. He was, for one thing, built like a toad, round in the middle and thin at the top and the bottom. His legs looked like toad legs, and his eyes even bulged.

I knew such thoughts were not Christian, but I did not feel very Christian sitting in the keeping room with Mr. Hezekiah pacing back and forth and Miss Crandall and Miss Almira perched on chairs near the hearth.

"Are thee ready, Mary?" he asked.

"Yes sir." He was going to use the Quaker thee and thou. I suppose I should be honored, but all it did was serve to put me off. Of course I was not ready. I was more ready for the judgment of the Lord Himself this cold February morning. Oh, why had I allowed Mama to stuff me with buckwheat cakes to keep my strength up? Why were my hands sweating when my feet were cold?

Why was my sister Sarah sneaking into the room and crouching in the corner?

"Very well." He stopped pacing and sat. "Since thee submitted thyself to this school and to the teachings of my sister, what would thee say was the one most important thing thee has learned?"

A trick, surely. And I'd stayed up half the night studying geography and sums! My head ached, my ears buzzed, my mouth was dry searching for words.

"To behave in a decent manner to all people, no matter their circumstances," I said. "To observe cleanliness and modesty and obedience and sobriety at all times. To live in harmony with all God's creatures, to tell no lie, to speak ill of no one, to return no injury, but practice forgiveness."

"Thee is a Quaker, then?"

"No, sir, but those are the rules of the school."

He nodded. "What is the name of the new vice president?"

This sudden turnaround gave me pause. But I quickly recovered. "Martin Van Buren."

His eyes seemed to go a little larger. "Who was President Jackson's opponent in the last election?"

I caught Miss Crandall's eye and she nodded encouragingly. "John Quincy Adams."

"What song was played when the British surrendered to the Americans at the end of the Revolutionary War at Yorktown?"

How many days had I sat wondering why I had to study a history of music? "The World Turned Upside Down," I answered.

He leaned back in the chair, crossed one frog leg over the other, and jiggled his foot. "Ah, one of my sister's favorite subjects is music. Does thee think such knowledge is useless, Mary?"

"I did, sir, but I don't think such now."

"And why is that?"

"Because I can answer you proper-like and not feel ignorant."

More jiggling of the leg. "What does thee intend to do with the education thee receives here?"

"I haven't thought on it, sir. Only what I will do if the school fails."

"And what is that?"

I wanted to say I would work in the mills with my sister Celinda. But he owned a cotton mill. He was, as Miss Crandall often said, "brisk for business." He might not take kindly to Celinda's passing as white. "Be a servant in a house of quality, sir," I said.

"And does thee think thy education will serve thee as thee removes dust and cobwebs from corners?"

I felt my face burn with shame. "My father says education serves everyone. He says one must learn for the sake of learning, sir. And that it is never a waste."

"And what if the school does not fail?"

"Then I shall think on it sir. But right now I only know it is important not to be ignorant."

"Does thee know what cities in America are larger than Boston?"

"New York and Philadelphia."

"What is the third largest place in Massachusetts?"

"Newburyport."

"What was the name of the Negro man who killed Major Pitcairn on Bunker Hill?"

"Peter Salem, sir. Only it wasn't Bunker Hill. It was really Breed's Hill."

He scowled. "Does thee correct me, then?"

"Yessir. But in the true spirit of humility. It is a common error and scarce an important one."

"All errors are important. If a girl makes an error in my mill she could lose a hand. Who is the king of England?"

"William the Fourth."

"Why was Sir Thomas More beheaded?"

"Because he refused to acknowledge Henry the Eighth as supreme head of the church."

"Who wrote *Gulliver's Travels?*"

"Jonathan Swift."

The frog's eyes were bulging now. "Can thee play the pianoforte?"

"I'm learning, sir. I'm not very good at it yet."

He stood up. He inclined his head. It was not a bow, but it was an acknowledgment of some sort. "Thee may go, Mary. I thank thee."

Before I left Sarah spoke up. "Sir, I would have thee quiz me also. I have a purpose for being here. I am going to use my education to teach children of color."

"Ah," Mr. Hezekiah said. "The famous Sarah. The one my sister will never give up."

Sarah beamed and curtsied. "Yessir. And I will do anything to convince thee of the importance of this school."

"Then perhaps, Sarah, thee will leave the room," he said, "so I can be alone with my sisters."

I fled to my room, as much to escape the wrath I knew would rain down on me from Sarah as my own terror. Had I failed? Surely his manner had changed from gruff to benign in the course of the interview, but did that mean anything at all?

I lay on my bed, spent from lack of sleep, and was soon dozing. In a short while there was a knock on my door and it opened. Miss Crandall stood there.

"Mary, dear, I couldn't wait a minute longer to tell you. Mr. Hezekiah has given me his backing!"

I sat up, dazed and confused.

Miss Crandall came in to sit on my bed. "He said you were not only quick and smart, but your intelligence was tempered with proper modesty. And if this was what I intended to accomplish with the other misses of color he would stand with me, not only as a Quaker and a brother but as a man of property and standing. And by doing so, others would follow. And not only that"—she hugged me, beaming—"he ordered—yes, ordered—Miss Almira to stand by me, too. Of course Miss Almira does everything Mr. Hezekiah and Mr. Reuben ask. He even gave permission for me to conduct proper meetings, as long as no male officiates. Oh, Mary dear, you have utterly convinced him, when I couldn't, that this undertaking is not only right, but necessary!"

"I'm glad I did well for you, Miss Crandall."

"There is still the town meeting, of course," she said. "But with Mr. Hezekiah behind me I am confident. I can't thank you enough, Mary. You don't know what your recitations meant to me this day. If half my pupils are like you, I shall know I am doing God's work."

I felt no gladness or pride. I felt, instead, foreboding. The future of the school had depended upon me. Mr. Hezekiah had not needed to hear from Sarah, only me. And he was a man to be reckoned with. Oh, why hadn't I appeared stupid? Or vain? Vanity would have put Mr. Hezekiah off. How stupid I truly was. I could have failed, given the wrong answers, and it all would have stopped here. This day. But now it would go on. And I knew in my bones that whatever befell us, it would not be good.

Chapter Eleven

⟿◇⟾

For some reason that had nothing to do with my wanting it, I got to go to the dreaded town meeting. It was my brother Charles who wanted to go, and Mariah with him. Secretly, Miss Crandall wanted to go too, but she was advised not to by Mr. Arnold Buffum and Reverend Samuel Joseph May. Mr. Buffum was the president of the New England Anti-Slavery Society. He also manufactured hats. Reverend May was another abolitionist who lived in Brooklyn, Connecticut.

They stood in our keeping room. "It would not behoove you, as a lady, to speak for yourself," said Mr. Buffum. "We are here to speak for you."

"Then I must write you both letters of introduction. Mary! My pen and paper!"

"Real abolitionists in our house!" I heard Sarah whisper to Mariah as I ran past them in the hall. "But I'm disappointed! I thought abolitionists would look different from regular folk."

Mr. Buffum and Reverend May both wore gray frock coats

and heavy wool coats with capes because of the cold. They were swathed in mufflers and wore spectacles. They looked like any of a dozen other men on Canterbury's streets.

When I returned with paper and pen I saw, out one of the front windows, a small crowd of town folk gathered outside our front gate. "What do they want?" Sarah ran to the front door.

"To see the abolitionists," I told her. "Just like you. Most people in Canterbury have never seen one before."

Quickly she turned to me. "Oh, and you have?"

"I've met Mr. Garrison." I felt smug.

"Well, then I think you should stay home from the meeting and let me go."

"Miss Crandall says she needs you to stay with her tonight."

"That's just because she doesn't want me being made a spectacle of." Sarah turned from the door, nose in the air. "They would mob me if I were there. Being that I am at the center of this fight."

I brought the paper and pen to Miss Crandall. A short while later Charles came to fetch me and Mariah and we followed Mr. Buffum and Reverend May across the green and up the hill to the Congregational Church. It seemed like half the town was headed there too.

"A meeting on Saturday night," Charles said. "This in itself bespeaks urgency. They go against their own law that no work or business be conducted between sundown on Saturday and sunrise on Monday."

The church held a thousand people. We made our way

through carriages, chaises, carts, even wagons, to climb the stairs in the vestibule to the gallery where people of color sat. Once up there I saw a sea of hats and bonnets, and the chatter and whispers sounded like a flock of crows. I was squeezed between my brother Charles and a post. "What are you doing?" Charles asked as I pulled some paper from my reticule.

"Making notes for Miss Crandall."

Charles was gentle and seemed blessed with a subdued wisdom. He had an affable manner, was well spoken and well read. "No, no, do not let anyone see you making notes. It could lead to trouble. They don't know you are one of Miss Crandall's girls."

Miss Crandall's girls. Was I tagged, then? I looked around. Several people had past sidelong glances at me and Mariah as we'd come in. I'd thought they were talking of Mariah and Charles, who looked so fine together. Everyone knew them as a betrothed couple.

At that moment a young man was making his way toward us, a white man, well dressed. He knew Charles. "Hello, Henry." My brother moved over, making room so he could sit between us. Henry couldn't have been more than twenty, and immediately he opened a leather case, took out notebook, quill pen, and bottle of ink. He set them all down on a leather case on his lap. Charles introduced him to Mariah and me.

"This is Henry Benson from Brooklyn," he said. "His father is Miss Crandall's friend."

"Why is he allowed to write?" I asked Charles.

"Don't be rude, Mary. He's writing the story for *The Liberator*," Charles said.

"I'm sorry," I said to Henry Benson, "but my brother won't let me write. I wanted to make notes for Miss Crandall."

"You can help me, and I'll share my notes with you," he whispered.

"How?"

"Well, I'm a stranger here. You can identify some of these people for me. For instance, what's the name of the moderator who's banging the gavel for order?"

I peered through the balcony railing to the deacon's seat. "Mr. Ashael Bacon. The man next to him is Mr. Judson, the lawyer. He's the one who's leading the fight against Miss Crandall."

"Good girl. How fortunate I am to be sitting next to you. You're one of the girls in the school, aren't you?"

I hesitated. "Yes. But people don't know it yet. They only know about my sister Sarah. So I don't think I want to be in your story."

"Smart girl, too. I shall honor your request. Charles, why didn't you tell me you had such a lovely, smart sister."

"I'm surrounded by lovely smart sisters," Charles said. "If she gets saucy, you let me know."

From that moment on I helped Henry Benson all night. When Mr. Judson got up to speak and said the idea for a school for "nigra girls" across the street from him was "insupportable," I told him how Mr. Judson was considered a gentleman of standing in town. I pointed out the Board of Visitors. When Reverend May and Mr. Buffum passed their letters from Miss Crandall to Mr. Judson, letters that introduced them and said they were acting for her, and Mr. Judson threw them down and bellowed that the two were not wanted in town, I reminded him that Mr. Judson wanted to be governor of Connecticut.

Nobody in the meeting would let Mr. Buffum or Reverend May speak. They were shouted down every time they tried. They were screamed at, threatened, and even cussed at.

"Men and women of Canterbury, I have come to have a word with you. Hear me out!" Reverend May jumped on a pew and waved his hat. "I am a minister of God. Never have I had to beg to be heard in a church!"

This brought some measure of quiet. Reverend May told them then to allay their fears. That Miss Crandall's school had no purpose other than education. "It will not be a center for abolitionists," he promised.

"It brought you here, didn't it?" someone yelled out. Then everyone laughed and commenced booing him.

"What we need to do," the same voice cried out, "is buy the house back from the old biddie and have her move the school."

"I do not wish the school anyplace in this town," Mr. Judson bellowed. He was very good at bellowing.

"Then we need to resurrect the old 1650 law. Bring it back on the books!"

"Yes," the crowd chimed in. "The 1650 law! The 1650 law!"

Henry Benson leaned over to me. "What law is this?"

"I don't know."

He asked Charles, but Charles didn't know either. Then a Negro man behind us who looked as if he'd been around since 1650 spoke up. "It's the law that prevents any foreigners from being chargeable to the town," he said.

"Foreigners?" Henry asked.

The old Negro man nodded. "Foreigners, son," he asserted. "As I recollect, it means no strangers can stay in the village for long unless the town authorities agree to it."

Henry recommenced writing. Below, the arguing went on, with one voice being heard above the others every so often. The word "vote" was now being bandied about. Then Mr. Judson's voice again. "Yes, we must vote on the 1650 law! Let us do so in the best tradition of the New England town meeting."

Applause. Henry stopped writing, put away his tablet, pen, and ink and nudged Charles. "If you don't mind my saying so, friend, this is the worst town meeting I've ever attended. It gives the tradition a bad name. I'm going for a bit of air. Do you mind if I take your sister with me? I don't think I'll be coming back. I've seen enough. I'd like to get the feelings of the ordinary folk in town. So I can walk your sister back to the school if you wish."

Charles agreed and Henry and I made our way downstairs and out into the frosty air. There, just below the church steps, others were crowded, voicing their disgust of the whole affair.

"Are you a reporter?" A young man approached us. I

recognized him as George White, the tanner, though he looked strange without his leather apron.

Henry introduced himself.

"Well, let me tell you, then, those people in there have lost their senses. They make me ashamed," said George White.

Henry sat down on the church steps, took out his tablet, pen, and ink and waited.

"That old 1650 law was never meant to shut down a school. And never meant to be used against a good Christian woman like Miss Crandall," George White said. "I tried to tell them that inside but they threatened me with bodily harm."

He agreed to be quoted, gave his name and occupation, then looked at me. "You're one of Mr. Harris's girls, aren't you?"

When I said I was he took off his hat, held it in his hands, and looked at me. "I want to apologize for those people in there, miss," he said. "They make me ashamed."

I thanked him. Then just as he turned to go off into the night two men from town walked by. One had a flask in his hand. "Heard what you said there, Mr. White," the one with the flask sneered at him. "Mayhap to prove your point you'd just might want to wed one of those little nigra gals when they bring them here."

His companion laughed uproariously and they disappeared into the shadows, on their way to Bacon's tavern down the road.

"I've left my horse there," Henry told me. "So I'll be headed there myself soon's I take you home. I need to get more folks' views on this thing."

As we walked home on the frozen rutted road, toward the distant lights of the seminary, I thought how exciting it must be to be a man and go about writing stories for a newspaper. And I made bold to ask him, "How old are you, Mr. Benson?"

"Twenty-two."

"And is it wonderful to go about and meet all kinds of people and write their stories?"

"Quite wonderful," he agreed.

"Would Mr. Garrison someday take on a woman reporter, do you think? Even if she was of color?"

"I would hope that by the time you are grown there would be no more need for Mr. Garrison's newspaper. You see, he often says his goal is to put himself out of business."

"My daddy says that would never happen. Do you think if I studied hard in school and learned to write he would someday take me on?"

"It's always possible," he said. "I shall personally put in a good word for you."

I gave a little skip, near slipped and fell on the icy ruts, and he held my arm. "Then that's what I shall do if Miss Crandall's school works and I get my education."

He laughed, pleased. Then sobered. "And if it doesn't work? What shall you do then?" he asked.

So I told him. About Celinda and the mill in Massachusetts. And he did not laugh then, did not even talk anymore, as a matter of fact, as he walked me the rest of the way home.

Chapter Twelve

They passed the law that night at the town meeting. It prohibited peddlers, itinerant preachers, and strangers of any ilk. They brought disease, the law said. And infectious ideas.

I went home for another visit. Miss Crandall sent Mariah and Sarah home, too. She even sent Miss Almira to their father's farm for a few days. She needed to be by herself, he said. To pray, to fast, and reflect.

Everyone had something different to say about the law. Daddy said, "Now more of our young men will go west." I did not see what going west had to do with it, but I said nothing.

"It is not a good thing, that 1650 law," Mama said. She spoke as if she'd been around in 1650 and had felt the effects of it.

Charles said: "I shan't go west. I'll stay here and see things out to the bitter end."

Sarah said: "It will be just that, brother. Bitter." Then she thought more and said, "If I am a stranger of some ilk, if my ideas are infectious, let them come for me."

Daddy said: "Don't encourage it, daughter. Remember, you are there to get an education. And it is the only place right now where you can get one."

Stephen Coit, when I went to the store said: "This town is more backward than I ever gave it credit for being."

In his newspaper Mr. Garrison said: "To colonize these shameless enemies of their species in some desert country would be a relief and a blessing to society." Then he listed their names in large black type. Andrew T. Judson, Rufus Adams, Solomon Paine, Captain Richard Fenner, Dr. Andrew Harris.

Back at the seminary, to my delight a letter came to the house from Henry Benson, addressed to My Friend. I ripped it open, delighted. *I enjoyed meeting you. My story was carried as I wrote it, but Mr. Garrison's remarks that preceded it and his vilification of these men was not my idea. I have told him, with all due respect, that his remarks are awfully cutting. Now you see what newspaper work can be. I hope to meet you again soon. Your humble servant, Henry Benson.* It was my first letter from a young man. I showed no one.

Miss Crandall was in her bed with a severe headache when we returned. Mariah set about making her delicacies to eat and soaking rags in vinegar to hold to her head.

"I'll take over getting the new girls assigned to their classes," Miss Almira said. "I'll have everything ready when they arrive."

"No," her sister said. "I'd rather thee went to town and

asked about for a cook. I'm going to be needing a good woman once the girls arrive. It is too much for Mariah. And she has her studying."

"All I ever get to do is errands!" Miss Almira flounced out.

After she left the old house got quiet. George Fayerweather came to call and Miss Crandall gave permission for him and Sarah to go out walking. Mariah busied herself in the kitchen. I wandered around aimlessly. The house was too quiet. My footsteps echoed on the heartpine floors. The firelight cast ominous shadows from the hearths. It was as if we were waiting for something to happen.

Two things did happen. Mr. Pardon came. "Miss Crandall has taken to her bed," I told him. "She is feeling poorly."

"Take me to her," he said. He was a tall, rangy man with a beard and heavy brows that made him look like he was forever scowling. He frightened me with his severity. He came in tramping snow, sending Mariah into fits of cleaning. She followed us up the stairs with rags in hand mopping up the wet.

He stopped midstairs. "Be finished with this gathered-in thing. It disturbs my quietude."

Mariah ran. I think he frightened her, too.

Then he stood at the foot of Miss Crandall's bed. "I have tried to stay in the background, because this is a gathered in business," he told her. "It disturbs my quietude more than that girl following me around mopping up my footsteps."

Miss Crandall was not frightened by him. "I know, Pa. I'm sorry."

"Thee is never ill, daughter."

"I'm not ill now, Pa. Just allowing myself a sulk is all. Did thee read *The Norwich Courier*? It's right here." She lay the paper out on the bed. "They're going to boycott me. Judson and his followers have voted on it! The way America boycotted Great Britain in the Revolution!"

Mr. Pardon looked at the paper. "If thy cause is recognized as worthy as that of the Revolution, thee has already accomplished something, daughter."

"They say they won't sell me a morsel of food once my girls come! The only one who said he would is Stephen Coit."

"Thee taught him well when he was thy pupil, then. And thee will teach these new girls well. Come, stop sulking, daughter. Is thee not up to the fight?"

"Not at this moment, Pa. Where will I get food for my pupils?"

"Thee will never be in want as long as I am around," Pardon said.

"Oh, Pa!" For the first time in my life I saw Miss Crandall cry. Her father stepped forward, took her hand, then knelt beside the bed in silent prayer. I knelt too, out of respect. When he was finished he told her, "Stay in bed this day, then get thee on thy feet. Thee has friends in great plenty."

Before he left he looked at me. "Care for her," he said. Then he was gone.

Miss Crandall got out of bed the next day and the house was once more brightened.

Until Miss Almira found the note in my room from Henry Benson.

I came into my room to see her there holding it. "Where did you get this?" she demanded. She was no longer the spoiled, pouting little sister now, relegated to running errands. She stood proud and superior, lording it over me. I suppose she had to lord it over somebody.

"It came for me," I said. I did not ask her what she was doing in my room. She had been in it before. It grieved me, but I did not have the mettle to demand an accounting from the darling of the Crandall family.

"For you!" Her lip curled in scorn. "And why do you think it is for you? Is your name anywhere on it?"

"No, but it said 'to my friend.' I helped Henry Benson that night at the town meeting. He walked me home. He told me . . ." My voice faltered.

"He told you what?"

"That he would recommend me someday to Mr. Garrison, if I wanted to write for the newspaper after I got my education."

Her laugh was lilting. "You? Write for Mr. Garrison? You get ahead of yourself." She put the note in her pocket. "Mr. Benson is a fine-minded young newspaperman. He is white. And the son of the president of the New England Anti-Slavery Society. He was being nice to you. Likely he felt sorry for you."

My face flushed. There was a buzzing in my ears, a dryness on my lips. I could not reply.

"And this is exactly the sort of business that Mr. Judson and his friends are looking for. Do you not know that he has gone to the Colonization Society and accused my sister of promoting intermarriage between Negroes and whites? Do you not know that is the leading fear that spurs the actions of those against my sister?"

I felt faint.

"You show little concern for your teacher's efforts. You must never be friends with a white man, do you understand? Or you will bring about the ruination of this school!"

With that she started for the door. "Henry Benson comes this evening, as a matter of fact, to visit my sister. I shall get him aside and explain matters to him. I suggest that this evening you stay in your room."

Then she was gone. I sat down, my head throbbing. Oh, I was so humiliated I wanted to die! I wanted to run now from the house and never return! I remembered Henry Benson's concern, his gentle face. Feeling sorry for me? I was covered with shame. How could I have been so stupid, so proud, so confident?

When he came that night, I feigned sickness and stayed in my room. If Miss Almira ever told her sister of the note, of our friendship, I never knew. It was not mentioned again.

Chapter Thirteen

⇒◆⇐

Miss Almira never did find a cook and so as the time got closer for the arrival of the new girls, I told Miss Crandall about Mrs. Mallard. She was a neighbor of ours. She and her husband lived half a mile down the road and she often sent around her wondrous winter squash pudding or gingerbread. She made the best griddle cakes I ever tasted and I knew she had a copy of Lydia Maria Child's *American Frugal Housewife*. Few people had it in our village. I knew some women who passed it around.

Miss Crandall sent Miss Almira to her with a note, and in no time Mrs. Mallard replied. She'd be more than happy to see well to the ways of the seminary kitchen. Her children were gone and time hung on her hands. She soon came around.

The seminary had a James stove. Mariah and Sarah and I had never used it. We were afraid of the firebox. And it came with all kinds of contraptions. Since the kitchen still had the old kind of hearth, we used that instead. Mrs. Mallard took right to the James stove, however, and the night before the girls were to arrive she made us a supper worthy of Thanksgiving. She was a short, round woman of color with lots of graying hair, a sprightly step, and she always hummed while she worked.

Early on the morning of April 1, when the girls were to arrive, we noticed a crowd gathered outside on the green. Men, women, and children standing there in the rain all dressed in black, with not even a blue cravat or green ribbon to relieve the tedium.

Mariah and Sarah and I were nervous. Miss Crandall didn't hold with such feelings. She said trust in the Lord was all we needed. I thought we needed Sheriff Coit at the very least, to protect us. Because that crowd stayed there and stayed there like statues, never moving in spite of the rain. I found them onerous, even though Miss Crandall tried to prettify it by saying they were just curious. To me, it was like a scene from a dream.

Finally the carriages pulled up, one after the other. From nowhere, it seemed, Mr. Pardon and Mr. Hezekiah and George Fayerweather came to help. As the doors of the carriages opened and each girl stepped out, one of them was there to take her hand, to help her down, to retrieve the luggage from the top where it was roped on, to carry it in.

So much luggage. So many girls. So much confusion and so many greetings. I stood next to Miss Crandall and checked off their names on her list. From Philadelphia came Elizabeth Bustill, Elizabeth Henly, Joan Johnson, and Mary Elizabeth Wiles. From New York, Henrietta Biolt, Marion Carter, Jeruska Congdon, Theodosa DeGrasse, Polly Freeman,

Geraldine Marshall, Ann Peterson, Catherine Ann Weldon, Amila Wilder. From Griswold in our own state there was Eliza Glasko. It was said her father sold whaling implements for which he had received patents from the U.S. Patent office. Harriet Lamson came from New Haven. She was the ward of a reverend, a white abolitionist. From Rhode Island came Ann Eliza Hammond. She brought her little sister Sarah, who was only nine. And Elizabeth Smith. From Boston came Julia Williams and Amy Fenner.

Twenty girls of color. Some laughing, some crying, as they bade farewell to fathers and mothers, some solemn, some frightened.

All were darker-skinned than me and Sarah. Somehow, in their midst we stood out. When Miss Crandall introduced us, they thought we were her teachers and helpers.

I rushed to help Mrs. Mallard. I brought the platters of griddle cakes in from the kitchen, and though invited to sit at the table, I walked around the edges of the reception. All these girls knew who they were, I decided. They knew why they were here. What's more, they were proud of what they were and willing to fight for it.

Why wasn't I sure of myself as they were? Because I knew more about things, I decided. If they knew, they wouldn't be chatting and laughing so gaily.

Halfway through the reception came the thumps on the doors. One, two, three, loud and heavy. Miss Crandall's cup clattered in her saucer. Mariah got up to go to the hall, but

Miss Crandall stopped her. The men had gone home, we were a house of women. The chatter stopped.

Then came a shout from a distance. "If you don't know your place you'll have to be taught, Prudence Crandall!"

More thumps. One, two, three, four. What were they throwing?

"Everyone away from the windows!" Miss Crandall said. Immediately she started grabbing the arms of girls and leading them to the center of the room. "What is it?" one or two girls asked tremulously.

"Pesky boys," she replied. "We have a horde of them in Canterbury."

Over the girls' heads I caught Mariah's eye. Oh, the lie of it, I thought. And Quakers were not supposed to lie. After a while Miss Crandall said it was all right that we sit back down. "Mrs. Mallard, would you be so kind as to pour another round of tea? And get some more of those wonderful griddle cakes?" Her voice was a pitch higher than usual. I'd come to recognize the tone as a great effort to rein in her fear. She went to the hallway. From my seat on the bench of the pianoforte I could see her open the door cautiously, step outside, and then say, "Oh my!"

Everyone ran to the hall. "What is it, what is it?" There was a chorus of questions. Miss Crandall stood outside staring at the dark green door. It was smeared with globs of human and animal dung that dripped in the rain. The smell was worse than an outhouse.

Some of the girls started to cry. One or two gagged and looked ready to vomit. Mrs. Mallard came out. "Well, it's a lot of cleaning up to do, but we'd best get started," she said.

A tall girl by the name of Julia Williams stepped forward and said in a Southern drawl, "If y'all give me some rags, I'll help."

"No, I couldn't let you, child," Miss Crandall said.

"I'm not a child. I'm twenty-one. My mama was a slave in South Carolina."

"No reason why you should be now," said Mrs. Mallard.

"Then who should do the cleaning?" asked Julia Williams. "You have somebody heah who just cleans dung from the doors?"

I decided that I liked Julia Williams. She had a directness about her that was supposed to be a Yankee virtue, but that had been in short supply at the seminary of late. "I'll help, Mrs. Mallard," I said. "You do look spent." Then Eliza Glasko, whose father had become rich by inventing whaling implements, stepped forward, to be followed by others.

"It's buckets of water we need," said Mrs. Mallard. "We'll throw the water at the door, then sweep it off. It would be better if it was hot. And if you changed out of your good dresses."

In ten minutes we were at work, Mrs. Mallard, Julia, Eliza, and myself. Before it was over we were all laughing. But I noticed, in the melee, that my sister Sarah had not offered to help. Neither had Ann Eliza Hammond. They had found each other. I'd seen them, heads together, walking upstairs.

❋ ❋ ❋

A letter from Celinda, dated April 4, 1833.

Dear Mary: I was so happy to receive your last favor and hear the news of home. It just proves what Mama always said, that you don't have to travel afar to have adventures. How I wish myself in your situation. The sentiments of Miss Crandall sound so noble and generous.

I am sorry about the business with Henry Benson and Miss Almira. The curse we have to carry, dear sister, is that you, I, and Sarah have such light skin. It is what led me to come to work in the mill, and now that I am here I live in fear that someone will discover what they call the taint in my blood, and I will be dismissed.

At any rate, of course you should have confided in me. I can understand your unwillingness to do so with anyone at home. And now, dear sister, if you would permit it, I will confide in you. But you must promise never to divulge anything I say to Mama and Daddy or the others.

I am now working in the spinning room and tending four sides of warp spinning frames, each with 128 spindles. This is the normal work for one girl. The work is extremely difficult but the overseer says he never had a girl make better progress than I have. Still, I was paid only $1.50 last week after room and board charges and after they took out the pew rent for the local Methodist church they require me to attend of a Sunday. We must all go to church, it doesn't matter which, as long as the churches get their pew rent. The reason I lost money last week was because of the heavy runoff from spring rains, which caused the water levels to back up and block the waterwheel. The mill had to cease operation for three days. We take the loss.

Many girls complain, as they complain about the long hours. We work from 5:30 in the morning until 7 o'clock at night, with time out only for meals.

I tell you this, dear sister because in your last letter you expressed an interest in coming here if things do not work out at the seminary. You should know that any money you would make here is dearly earned. I have never worked so hard in all my born days, and many times I almost concluded to give up and return home. Besides which, it is very difficult to get a position. You have to start by being a doffer, the money is not good, and it takes at least six months before you have any frames of your own. I moved especially fast and made good progress.

Perhaps with me already here it will be easier for you. I shall certainly look out for your interests. And perhaps if you do come, things will be easier. What am I saying? For that to happen I and the other girls will have to work to make them that way. And that means organizing and making our needs known. I think it is coming to be that this is what we will have to do. I suppose I'm a lot like Daddy. I don't like controversy. But if need be, I will take part in it to better my lot, the lot of other girls here and those to come. Write soon.

Yours affectionately, Celinda.

Chapter Fourteen

That first week with the new girls was chaos. Or as near to chaos as one could arrive at in a house run by a Quaker lady. I thought it wrong of Miss Crandall to keep from the girls the true nature of our situation. But I told no one. I no longer confided in Sarah. Now that she, too, lived at the school, our late-night talks were over. She roomed with someone else. Besides, I think, given the nature of our feelings for one another these days, they would be over anyway.

I missed those talks. I had no one I could confide in now. So I kept my own counsel. Before that first week was over, however, I minded that the girls had a purchase on the situation. Even nine-year-old Sarah Hammond.

"Will you buy some bacon soon?" she asked one morning at breakfast.

That started it. "And eggs?" ask Harriet Lamson.

"How can she?" whispered Eliza Glasko. "I heard no one will sell to us."

The buzz started and went round the table, stopping only

when Miss Crandall rapped it with her knife. "Girls, girls everything is fine."

"How can it be fine," said Ann Eliza Hammond, "when less than a week ago they threw human excrement against the front door? The town folk don't want us here."

"They do," Miss Crandall insisted. "They are just Connecticut Yankees and find it difficult to accept strangers. Any strangers."

"Then why can't we walk to town?" asked Sarah Hammond.

"Because it's been raining for three days," Miss Almira answered for her sister. No lie there. Even the weather had not been accommodating.

"It's letting up now," said Elizabeth Smith. "Can't we go today?"

"Not today," Miss Crandall said, "but soon. We have Latin today."

Groans of commiseration. Through all of this I was watching Julia Williams. She had a curious smile on her face, but she said nothing. She was a silent one, seldom voicing an opinion but always watching.

After breakfast I helped clear. It was still my job because my tuition was free. I didn't mind. I enjoyed helping Mrs. Mallard in the kitchen. When I brought in a heap of dirty dishes I felt someone walking behind me, and turned to see Julia Williams.

"This isn't your job," I told her.

"I don't consider myself too high-toned. Unless you don't want the help."

I thanked her and smiled.

"I've sent word to my husband," Mrs. Mallard was saying. "Crops are new in the ground, but we have some dried foodstuffs stored in our attic—corn, apples, pumpkins, onions."

"But how long will they hold out?" I asked. "I never saw girls eat like these do."

She laughed. "They sure do eat. Does my heart good to see it. I heard Miss Almira say she was going to ask her pa to bring some food from his farm. Miss Crandall, she didn't like that one little bit. Oh, no, she's a proud one all right. They had high words about it, but Miss Almira won and sent word around to their pa."

"I know someone in town who will sell to us."

"Who?"

"Stephen Coit. Do you know him?"

She chuckled as she immersed the dishes in the tin basin. "Oh, I know him, all right. I know him. He's a good friend of my husband."

Something about the way she said it piqued my interest. But in the next moment I forgot, because Julia Williams was bringing in another stack of dirty dishes and Miss Crandall was calling both of us to class.

Before Latin I stopped her in the hall. "Miss Crandall, Stephen Coit will sell to us."

She was agitated, not wanting to admit her need. "That won't be necessary, Mary," she said.

"But it is, sister." Miss Almira came up with a load of Latin textbooks. "Let her go and ask him for some food. Wasn't he one of thy students at thy last school?"

"Yes."

"I thought I knew the name," mused Miss Almira.

"He's a friend of mine," I said. "He said if you ever needed anything for your school you could count on him. He told me that."

Miss Almira cast a knowing look at me. "A friend? How?"

"He's a friend of our whole family," I amended. "My daddy sells him produce."

It was decided that after classes I should go to Stephen's store. So I was given a basket and money and cautioned to take less frequented paths home.

"I live in this town," I told Miss Crandall. "People are accustomed to seeing me about."

"But you are a girl of color attending my school," she admonished. "Always remember that."

Somehow I knew I would never be able to forget it.

The Franklin stove in Stephen's store gave good heat in the April chill. "Of course I'll sell to Miss Crandall, Mary," he said. Then one by one he put the items in my basket. Fresh coffee beans, a bag of tea, a pound of cheese, molasses, a slab of bacon, flour, sugar, and the other "boughten" goods we'd need in the next day or two.

"So the others won't sell to you, hey?" he asked. "Well, I

always did say the people in this town were hypocrites, for all their pious talk against slavery."

Slavery. The word hung in the air between us. It got in the way of the smell of the pickles. But Stephen seemed not to be aware of the uncommon powers the word had on me.

"Miss Crandall's a good lady. I did so poorly with sums in school and she made me know how important they are. Now, every time I add a column of figures I think of her."

"Mrs. Mallard, our new cook at school, says she knows you," I told him.

His face had no expression. "Yes. They're good people. They trade their eggs here for olive oil, spices, and coffee. Doesn't she make the best griddle cakes?"

I said yes, but wondered how he knew it. "Tell her I'm her humble servant," he said. And when I left he gave me some taffy. "Take heart, Mary," he said. "I'm your friend."

Friend. Another word that got in the way of the smell of pickles. I thanked him and left.

What I had purchased dressed up our table for two days and Mrs. Mallard received it like it was manna in the Bible. "That dear boy. People don't know how good he is. His daddy wanted him to go on to college, you know. But he said no. He wanted to stay right here in Canterbury and run that store and get to know the people."

Mr. Pardon came late that afternoon in his wagon, with supplies from his farm. The girls came out the back door and crowded around him. Some of the girls from New York City squealed in delight at the "quaint New England farmer in Quaker gray." I waited for Miss Crandall to introduce him as her father. But she did not.

"Why didn't she?" I asked Mariah later.

"She does not wish them to know he is not a local merchant, that only one will sell to her. He has agreed to it. She does not wish to disquiet them."

I thought if it were my daddy I would introduce him. I would make them curtsy to him. Sometimes I just don't understand Quaker people. Sometimes I just don't understand white people at all.

But she could not keep from them the fact that they could not walk into town. They insisted. The sun was bright, the trees budding, daffodils' heads bobbing all around the house, birds singing, the girls young and full of briskness.

Finally on Saturday, the end of the first week, she relented. "We'll take a walk," she said. "But we go two by two, and walk decorously. Heads high. No talking. Hold hands. Come along, Mary."

"I have chores, Miss Crandall."

"Come along, I said. Quickly now. We need to make a favorable first impression with the good people of Canterbury."

I got into line. The one girl who did not have a partner was Julia Williams. She stayed apart, to herself, and did not seem to mind walking alone. When I stood next to her she smiled, then shrugged as if to say, "If we must, we must." We were last in the line, except for Miss Almira, who walked in back of us with a book open.

"Thank you for backing me when I offered to clean the door," she said.

"I thought you were very brave."

"My mama always says, 'Somebody got to step forward and be either brave or stupid.' I think now it was more stupid."

"It was brave," I insisted.

"I notice that sister of yours didn't offer."

"Sarah? No, she's waiting for the right moment to be a heroine. Like Joan of Arc."

"Well, we can't all be Joan. Some of us have got to clean the castle."

I liked her wit. "Two by two," I whispered to her, "like animals going into Noah's ark."

"Yes," she said, "and as I recollect the cause of that expedition was impending disaster."

"Hush, girls," scolded Miss Almira from behind. "We don't need that kind of talk. Now I wish to go and walk with my sister, but you must promise me first to behave."

Julia raised her eyebrows and rolled her eyes at me. "Yes, Miss Almira," she said with mock humility. Then she whispered to me, "Lordy, do I never get away from the overseer?"

We started walking. "Tell me about your mother who was a slave," I said.

She sighed. "What's to tell?"

"What was it like being a slave? Do you recollect?"

"I recollect, sure 'nuf. I was born in Charleston, South Carolina. Lived there until I was fifteen years old. My daddy came from a neighboring plantation. He wed my mama and when his master died he gave Daddy his freedom, providing he go North. They didn't want any free nigras around, give the other slaves notions. So Daddy went North, to Boston, and earned money to buy me and Mama from slavery."

"What's it like being a slave?" I asked. "All we hear is how we have to free our brothers and sisters who are in bondage. Miss Crandall is absolutely daft over the subject."

She was silent for a moment, in a black study. I thought she had not heard me. Then she smiled. "You want to trade secrets?"

"What?"

"Then we'll be friends. You tell me something you can't tell anybody else. An' I'll tell you something I know I'll never tell anybody 'round heah."

"Yes," I said.

"Good. You start."

I was taken aback for a minute, but the look in her brown eyes, which were flecked with gold, reached out to me. She wants to tell me something, I told myself. Something she can't tell anyone else. So I thought for a minute.

"Remember, it has to be important. Not just a no 'count secret," she urged. "You have to be able to trust me."

"All right. My sister Celinda passed as white and went to work in the mills in Lowell."

I saw the pupils of her eyes widen. "Nobody knows?"

"Only my parents, my sister, and the person who helped her get there." I thought of Mr. Begley, but decided he wasn't important enough to mention. Then I thought of Henry Benson, but decided to forget him.

She nodded solemnly, taken with the weight of it. Then she confided her secret to me. "I was whipped," she said.

For a moment I did not understand. Then I did. "When you were a slave?"

She nodded. "I have scars. I was whipped by the overseer where me and Mama lived. Right before my daddy bought our freedom."

My mouth went dry. "Why?" I asked.

"'Cause I wouldn't let him play free with me. It was all he wanted. Bothered me for near a year."

"Oh, Julia! I'm so sorry!"

She shrugged. "These girls here are spoiled. No eggs and bacon!" She scoffed. "I ate cornpone three times a day sometimes. They don't know what they have."

She went on to tell me how the little white daughter on the plantation had taught her to read; how, when her daddy brought them North, she went right into a school in Boston for girls of color.

"I'd admire to get into the Noyes Academy in Canaan, New Hampshire," she said. "It welcomes people of color. Men and women. I want to be a teacher."

We walked in silence a bit and I felt the warmth of

friendship spreading between us. "How can you abide even speaking of it?" I asked her.

"My mama reads a powerful lot. She says the Russian people tote a lot of miseries. And they have a saying. 'If'n you look back at everything, you lose the sight of one eye. But if'n you don't look back at all, you'll go blind.'"

I nodded and reached for her hand. Just to touch it.

We hadn't gotten within shouting distance of the stores and houses before the good people of Canterbury gave us their welcome.

The first rock almost hit little Sarah Hammond in the head. She was just ahead of us and it would have if Julia hadn't seen it coming and pulled Sarah down. The rock whooshed by, landed in the street, and skipped several times before stopping.

A few girls screamed, but Miss Crandall gathered them around her and hushed them.

"It's those pesky boys again," said Julia. "The same as put the manure on the door, I suspect." She held and soothed Sarah. "Or maybe," she mumbled so low that only I could hear, "it's the overseer."

The rock had come from behind a nearby fence in an open lot. A tall fence that shielded our assailants well. Whoever they were, they could throw. Stones followed. And clumps of mud that sometimes hit their mark. There was general mayhem as the girls shielded their faces and broke ranks.

"Girls, girls," came Miss Crandall's voice. "Stand firm! Don't let them frighten you!"

Standing firm was the last thing they intended to do. We ran, all of us, back toward the school. Skirts flapped, bonnets were lost, crying was heard, and above it all Miss Crandall's voice.

"Girls, girls! Walk in line!"

Julia grabbed the hand of little Sarah Hammond on one side and mine on the other and just about dragged us along.

"I live in this town!" I told her, panting. "I don't have to run."

"Honey, you want to stand and discuss it, go right ahead. But I'm not about to let that overseer get me."

Laughter from behind. Obscene catcalls, whistles, and shouts. It was a way back to the seminary, and I thought the pain in my side would cripple me. But Julia pulled me along. Once on the grounds, Miss Crandall faced us, hair straggling around her face, muddied skirts and all. "Girls, why didn't you stand firm? Why did you run?"

Nobody answered. Then Julia stepped forward. "I think, Miss Crandall, with all respect, you should have told us how ornery those town folk are. They're like a parcel of skunks on the prowl. You should have told us. Leastways we'd know what to expect."

The other girls murmured their agreement, and I felt a swelling of pride in Julia.

"You don't credit us with having the sense of hooty owls," she pushed.

"You can't speak that way to my sister." Miss Almira stepped forward to scold, but Miss Crandall held up her hand. "Let her continue," she said. "In this school we have open discussion and debate."

"You can't fight a war lessin' you know there is one," Julia finished in her low reverent voice.

Miss Crandall took no umbrage. "You're right, of course. I have been wrong. I apologize. We'll discuss it this evening after supper," she said.

Chapter Fifteen

O nce evil gets in through the door crack, my mama
always says, you're hard put to keep it out. And
that's what she said when I told her how no one
in town but Stephen Coit would sell us food.

"Evil is like the noxious night air," she said, "it finds its way
in. You tell that Miss Crandall your daddy will be selling her
his vegetables just as soon as the ground yields the first crop.
Just like we've always done. No need to change now."

"Miss Crandall says if we try to understand our enemies and
forgive them, we'll be all right," I told her.

"Does she, now? Well, you be careful just the same," Mama
cautioned.

I don't make a habit of spying. It isn't in my nature to
do such a thing. But two days after this I brought some
tea, at her request, to Miss Almira at her desk in her
room. It was just after I set the tray down that I saw
the heading on the letter she was writing.

Dear Mr. Garrison, it read.

It was a very long letter and it had the look about it of being very important. Farther down on the page I caught sight of the words *storekeepers,* and *supplies,* and *disgusting matter on the front door.*

Why does she write Mr. Garrison? I wondered. He is an acquaintance of Miss Crandall's.

The day after, we were at the noon meal, chatting away, when of a sudden Eliza Glasko started choking and gagging and getting red in the face.

Miss Crandall was not in the room. Miss Almira was. "Prudence," she yelled, "Prudence, come quickly. We need you!"

In her excitement she'd forgotten to use the Quaker "thee." Miss Crandall came running. By the time she got there, though, Julia Williams, who was seated next to Eliza, had stood up and knocked the glass of water from Eliza's hand. It crashed to the floor. Then Julia grabbed Eliza and bent her over. "Spit it out!" she ordered. "Puke it up!"

Eliza did, right there on the Persian carpet in the dining room. In a minute Miss Almira was on Julia. "What are you doing to her?"

"The water!" Julia said. And she picked up her own glass and thrust it at Miss Almira. "Look at it. Smell it. Don't taste it. It's poisoned."

It was then that we noticed that the water in the glasses was cloudy, with something in it that was settling to the bottom.

I'd been just about to take a sip when Eliza started gagging.

"It's true," Miss Crandall pronounced. "But how did you know, Julia?"

Julia gave no response. But I knew. She was always on the alert for that overseer, knowing that somehow, somewhere, he would strike at her again.

My daddy and Mr. Pardon brought water that very night. Barrels of it. And again that night Miss Almira requested a cup of tea made with the good water be brought to her room. She was writing another letter. Again I saw the salutation at the top: *Dear Mr. Garrison.*

There are those who will think I am being ungrateful and going above my station for writing what I am about to write. But I had the feeling that spring that the evil inside that old Paine mansion was worse than the evil attacking us from outside.

Miss Almira was writing to Mr. Garrison on the sly, reporting to him all that was going on in the seminary, all the attacks. Just like she'd used to report to Mr. Reuben. It made no difference to whom she reported, it seemed. Miss Almira pined to be important. All she'd been allowed to do here at the seminary was run errands. Not teach classes. Some people will do anything just to be important.

Within a week the latest copy of *The Liberator* carried the full story of how only one merchant in town would sell to us, and they named him, Stephen Coit. The story also told how filthy matter had been thrown against our dignified front door and how our well had been poisoned.

Miss Crandall cried when she read it. Then she gathered me and Sarah, Mariah, and her sister into the keeping room.

"Someone is talking," she told us. "This newspaper account never should have happened. We only incur more wrath."

"Mayhap it is one of the girls innocently writing home," my sister Sarah suggested.

Miss Crandall considered this for a moment. "Most likely," she sighed. "But I shall write to Mr. Garrison and request that he keep such distressing news under wraps."

As I left the room I looked straight into Miss Almira's eyes. They were as innocent as a newborn babe's.

"So, I heard my name got in *The Liberator*." Stephen Coit reached for some oranges and lemons and put them in my basket. Then a cone-shaped loaf of sugar wrapped in purple paper.

"Yes. No one knows how, but we suspect an informer in the house," I told him.

"An informer." He measured some flour and put it in a sack. "Well, it makes sense when you think about it."

"It does?" I cast a quick surprised look at him. "Why?"

"Why not? Think of the opportunity here on all sides. That school is like fruit for the picking for the abolitionists. And someone inside wants not only their backing but the notoriety they will gain from it. Do you need any coffee today?"

"Yes. The usual amount. Aren't you fearful people will retaliate because you sell to us?" I asked him.

"They daren't, with my father being the sheriff."

"And how does your father feel about it, then?"

"He does his job and I do mine. He's staked me in this store, so he has an interest in it, too. And speaking of my father, Miss Mary, he's a good man. Anything he does in connection with that school he does because it is his sworn duty, not because he enjoys it. Remember that."

"Is he about to do something I should know about?" I asked.

"Just remember it," he said again. Then he gave me some taffy and I left.

Perhaps I was the only one in the house not surprised that evening when the sheriff stood at the green front door.

We were at supper. A supper that had started with a prayer by Miss Crandall, that each and every one of us forgive the merchants in town who would not sell to us, as well as Mr. Garrison for writing his harsh account of our troubles.

It was raining again and the sheriff stood there, mud splattered, his horse waiting. "Miss Crandall?" he asked.

"You know me perfectly well," she said.

"I have a writ."

Miss Crandall sighed.

"I'd like to read it now, Miss Crandall."

"Yes, do," she replied.

By now we were all in the hall, crowding around her. Outside the rain poured down. The sheriff took a paper from his coat pocket and commenced to read.

"Based on the old pauper law it has been decreed that Ann Eliza Hammond, who hails from Providence, Rhode Island, and has taken up residence in Canterbury, Connecticut, is hereby declared a foreigner. As such she must leave the village of Canterbury or be fined $1.67 a week. If she does not comply she will be sentenced to be whipped on the naked body, not exceeding ten stripes."

From behind me came exclamations of fear.

"Why is Ann Eliza the only foreigner? Many of my girls come from other places," Miss Crandall asked.

"It was determined she was the first girl of color to arrive at the school," the sheriff said.

"Indeed. Well, Sheriff, which one of you determined that I do not know. But Sarah Harris was my first girl of color. You have gotten your facts confused already."

"Yes, yes, I was here first." I turned to see my sister push through the crowd. "I shall be the one whipped, though I live in town. And thank the Lord who has brought me to this day."

"No, he named me," said Ann Eliza.

"Enough," Miss Crandall said. "Sheriff, I know you only do your duty. You are soaked to the skin. May I offer you something hot to drink?"

The sheriff folded up the paper and put it back in his

pocket. "No, ma'am, I have to be off. But I'll tell you, they aren't shilly-shallying, these people. I wouldn't take it lightly."

"Thank you. I assure you we take it in all seriousness," Miss Crandall told him. And she closed the door.

As you can expect, there was no peace in the house all that evening. Supper was scarce eaten before Miss Crandall called for a general discussion, which soon collapsed into an argument between Sarah and Eliza Ann over who should be whipped.

In the middle of it Julia Williams got up, excused herself, and left the room. No one paid mind. Both Ann Eliza and Sarah considered themselves Joan of Arc, it seemed. I could not believe my sister Sarah. Whatever change had come over her since she had come to this school, I could not resolve it with the sister I once knew.

"We must not let turmoil reign in this house," Miss Crandall said. "And remember, we have important friends in the community. They will not permit this to happen."

She did not name them, however. But the next day we found out what our enemies were capable of. And the next day Mr. Reuben came to visit.

Chapter Sixteen

———◆———

The dead cat was hanging from a tree in the front yard. I recognized it as the handsome black-and-white that roamed the area, the one we'd fed on occasion.

There was something so sad in seeing it hanging there. And so ominous.

Mr. Reuben found it when he came up the front walk. He stopped to cut it down, then having done so, was not sure exactly what to do with it. He stood there holding it and looking at Miss Crandall as she stood in the doorway.

"There is a note with it," he said.

"Read it," she instructed.

"'Dear Schoolteacher,'" he read. "'This is what happens when black and white are mixed together. While everyone in Canterbury abhors the horrible traffic in slavery, we see no need for the State of Connecticut to educate Negroes from other states. It is well known that colored people in the midst of a white population are an appalling source of crime and pauperism. The immense evils of such a situation can only be stopped by timely intervention.'"

Mr. Reuben set the cat down on the front steps. "Sister, I hope thee is going to take warning from this."

Miss Crandall smiled. "I am not."

"Well then, let me say that I have come with every intention to break up this school. It is bringing disgrace down on our family."

Mariah ushered me and two other girls into the kitchen. The remaining girls were studying upstairs. Mrs. Mallard was brewing tea. We sat at the table. I could hear not actual words, but the tone of them. Miss Crandall and her brother carrying their argument into the parlor, pulling it back and forth between them like taffy, stretching the truths of it and rearranging the lies.

"Father has already been warned to stay away from thy school. Or he will be sued." From Mr. Reuben.

"He has gone to the selectmen." From Miss Crandall.

"They have turned their back on him." From him. "Father is getting on. He enjoys a position of eminence in this community. Is it right to mar his elderly years with insults and ill remarks from people he calls neighbors?"

"No." From Miss Crandall. "But then the neighbors should stop. Are thee sure it's Father thee is concerned with, Reuben?"

"And who else should I be concerned with, then?"

"Thyself."

"Prudence! When will thee grow up? Thee cannot succeed

here. All thee is doing is feeding the needs of the aboli-tioist!"

"And how, may I ask, does thee know what I am doing, liv-ing all the way in Peekskill?"

"I read it in Mr. Garrison's newspaper!"

They went on like that for the better part of an hour behind closed doors in the front parlor, voices rising and falling, while we pretended to be interested in our tea. "My," Mrs. Mallard said, "I never knew Quakers argued so. All that thee-ing and thouing can sure fool a person."

Every once in a while one of us would wince as the voices from across the hall got especially loud. I have to laugh when I hear today how people spoke of us, the colored inhabitants of Miss Crandall's seminary after this whole business was over. They said we were mild-mannered young misses who all went quietly about their business while the turmoil raged outside the Paine mansion.

The turmoil inside was worse. Because inside the girls were dividing into two factions, with my sister Sarah and Ann Eliza heading up one and Julia Williams and myself heading up the other, although at first I didn't know I was heading up any-thing. I didn't want to head up anything. But we don't always get to do or not do things as we wish in this world. And so it was that I got to be adjunct of the Study Bodies, the name Julia gave to our group. Julia said an adjunct is one who helps out the leader. Julia also said the most important lessons we were going to learn at this school would not be from books.

It had started the night before, after Sheriff Coit left. Immediately several of the girls ran upstairs to congregate in the room Sarah shared with Ann Eliza. Those of us who knew we were not wanted stood outside in the hall. "What do you suppose is going on?" I asked.

"They're deciding who is to get whipped first," Julia Williams said. Her voice had contempt in it. And a deadness only I recognized.

Eliza Glasko agreed. "They have come here not to learn but to be part of a cause. They have come to make trouble. I sometimes think Mr. Garrison sent girls from certain families for this purpose. They call them agitators. Their history goes all the way back to the Boston Massacre in this country."

Was this true? Had certain girls come to this school just to stir up trouble? I recollected studying about the Boston Massacre in history. "They said that Crispus Atticus was an agitator," I told the others.

"Right, he was," said Eliza. "Now you all know what I mean, then."

"But what about Miss Almira? What is her part?" asked little Sarah Hammond. For some reason her older sister had not included her.

"For the glory of it," said Julia. "They are all so taken with vanity."

"Yes," I agreed. "I know that Miss Almira's been writing letters to Mr. Garrison. I saw them."

Julia groaned. "And so that's how he knows everything going on heah, then." She was getting more vexed by the minute, pacing, arms folded across her bosom. "I declare! A parcel of hound dogs makes more sense than they do!" She blurted out finally, "Don't they know not to play with fire?" And with that she stepped up to the closed door and rapped soundly three times.

In a moment it opened a crack. "Go away, can't you see we're busy?" asked Ann Peterson.

She was a New York girl, and they considered themselves superior to everyone else. All the New York girls were in that room, invited.

"You all busy doing what? Not studying, I wager," said Julia.

"How do you know?"

At that Julia pushed the door. She was a tall thin girl, but strong, and she soon was inside the room where the girls were sprawled on two beds and on the floor. Miss Almira was at her desk.

"Now just one minute," she said, getting up.

"No, you all give me one minute." Oh, I was so proud of Julia, the way she stormed into that room, like an avenging angel, and stood there tall and straight, and unafraid. "You all think it's a frolic, being whipped? It's worse than a hog-killing. That's what you feel like, a strung-up hog with its skin being ripped off!"

"How do you know, Julia?" Ann Eliza said teasingly. "Oh, I forgot, you come from a plantation. I suppose you're going to give us tomfoolery about slaves being whipped and you watching."

"No. I didn't watch," Julia said quietly. "Everybody else watched, while they did it to me."

And with that impossible pronouncement, she turned her back to them, looking at us in the hall. "One of you all out there come in and unbutton my dress in back, will you?"

We stood mute, staring.

"Mary? Will you come in and help me? So they don't think I'm just caterwauling?"

I bestirred myself and went to her and commenced to unbutton the dress. I struggled with the buttons, my hands trembling, while everyone waited. When I finished, Julia pulled her dress down over her shoulders, revealing her back.

Everyone gasped and the girls in the hall came in to look, too. I had my eyes squeezed shut, then I opened them. I looked at Julia's back.

It was scarred with terrible welts. I felt dizzy, and some of the girls even backed away.

"Who did that?" Ann Eliza asked.

Holding her dress in front at the shoulders for the sake of modesty, Julia answered. "The overseer on the plantation. Because I wouldn't allow him to put his hands on me. Button me, Mary."

I did so with shaking fingers.

"I tell you all, when you feel that lash you won't be so happy." Julia turned to face them. "Nobody deserves such treatment. Not even a dog. Remember that while you all plan your great moment!" And she ran from the room.

In the hall outside she wept and covered her face with her hands while the girls comforted her. I stood aside, horrified at the sound of her bitter tears.

"Do the scars hurt?" little Sarah Hammond asked.

Julia said no. But I knew that the scars were not only on her back. But inside her. And yes, they did hurt. All the time.

The girls in Miss Almira's room went on with the meeting.

Afterward I sat with Julia in her room. Little Sarah Hammond went downstairs to fetch some tea. When she came back she had news. "I listened outside the door. They're going to call themselves the Paines." She set the tea down. "My mama wouldn't like Ann Eliza doing this."

"Why the Paines?" Julia asked.

"It has two meanings," I said. "They consider themselves patriots like Tom Paine. And it carries the name of this mansion."

"We'll have to find a name for ourselves," Sarah Hammond suggested. "I'll talk to the other girls who are not allowed in their group."

"Why?" Julia asked. "Why do we have to?"

Sarah Hammond eyed us solemnly. "If we don't, we'll be left out," she said with all her nine-year-old wisdom. "We can't let that happen. Or it will be just like before we came here, being shut out of things. We can't let that happen, can we?"

"No, sweetie," Julia said. "We can't let that happen at all."

"But what will we stand for?" I asked. "If they are patriots, what are we?"

"We'll stand for everything they aren't," Sarah purposed. "And we are the opposite of everything they are."

Then she went to bed, leaving us to ponder the matter.

The next day before Mr. Reuben left he asked Miss Almira to go with him.

We had been studying Shakespeare's *Merchant of Venice*, and just as we got to the scene when Portia tells Nerissa that her little body is aweary of this great world, the door opened and Mr. Reuben stood there. Miss Almira was sitting in on the class.

"Almira," he said, "I wish thee to come with me. I can no longer do anything about our sister. But I still have a chance to remove thee from the trouble around here."

There was a moment of silence. Miss Almira became flushed in the face. And I thought, How little you know, Mr. Reuben. She loves the trouble. And I delighted in Miss Almira's predicament, because I knew she also delighted in her brother's indulgence.

But her predicament only lasted a moment. Until one or two girls said, "Oh no, don't go, Miss Almira, don't go. How shall we fare without you?" They belonged to the Paines, of course.

It pleased her vanity. She looked at Mr. Reuben. "Darling

Reuben," she said. "Can't thee see how these girls need me? How can I run out on my obligations? Thee wouldn't want me to dishonor our Quaker beliefs, would thee?"

"Of course not, dear," Mr. Reuben said. "But thee knows where I am if thee needs me."

Miss Almira got up then and ran to him, into his arms. He embraced her and left. And I thought, Miss Almira is playing it both ways. It isn't fair. But some people can, I have found. They can play it both ways and never lose. I have also found out that I am not one of them.

Chapter Seventeen

They buried the cat the next day, the Paines. They built a small coffin for it and sang over its grave the backyard. They sang a hymn over a cat! Miss Crandall, who as a Quaker knew about persecution and believed in allowing everyone their own beliefs, accepted it.

She looked out the window in the kitchen and shook her head sadly. "I suppose we must permit them their grief," she said, "although it is only a cat."

"It isn't grief," Mariah made bold to tell her.

"What is it, then?" Miss Crandall asked.

But Mariah was not that bold. "The girls who are going to walk to church in Packerville are ready in the hall, Miss Crandall" was all she said.

"And the others? Those burying the cat? Aren't they coming to church?" Miss Crandall asked.

Mariah didn't answer. Neither did I. Miss Almira, who had just come in the door, did. "The girls who are burying the cat wish to go across the green and stand in front of the doors of the Congregational Church until they are allowed inside, sister," she said.

Miss Crandall was considerably confused. "They closed their doors against us last Sabbath."

"Which is why they wish to go and stand in front of them today." Miss Almira spoke carefully, as to a child.

"That is not keeping the Sabbath," Miss Crandall said. And I felt sorry for her then, because everybody in the house seemed to know what was going on but her. She had started this school for her own reasons, and everyone had taken those reasons and turned them inside out and upside down to fit their own purposes. And nobody had told Miss Crandall about it. Nobody at all.

Julia stepped in from the hall then and made some attempt to tell her. "I don't hold with what they want. But they'd rather stand outside this church than go in the one in Packerville," Julia said gently. "That's the way of it with those girls out there burying that cat."

"And the way of the girls in the hall?" Miss Crandall asked.

"They want to go to church," Julia said.

"Am I to surmise, then, that my girls are divided into two different groups? That want two different things?"

"Yes, ma'am, you are correct," Julia allowed.

Miss Crandall sighed, looked once more out the window, and then glanced at her sister.

"And thee? What does thee wish?" she asked.

"To stand with the girls who go across the green," Miss Almira said.

I saw the disappointment shadow Miss Crandall's face. "I did not wish the means to become more important than the end," she said.

"It cannot be avoided, sister. Thee has set certain actions in motion."

"But to be divided in our methods . . ." Miss Crandall's voice dropped away.

"Does it matter how we arrive at the purpose? As long as we arrive there?" Miss Almira asked. "And if some take a different road to get there, is that bad?"

"I only know I do not wish my students working against each other!" Miss Crandall's voice grew shrill. "Look at those girls out there." She turned to me. "Why are you and the others not with them?"

"They don't want us with them," I stammered. "What they want is not what we want."

"And what is that?" she demanded sharply.

I wanted to cry. Never had she raised her voice to me.

Julia stepped forward then. "They want to be whipped. For the sake of making a name for themselves. We do not."

"That is not true," Miss Almira argued. "They say only that they hope to have the mettle to take the whippings in Miss Crandall's name. They are brave and dear. Do not speak ill of them."

"No one will be required to take whippings," Miss Crandall said stoutly. "I promise them that."

"Then thee has come up with the money to pay the fines, sister?"

Miss Crandall faltered. "No."

"And those fines must be paid weekly now. And we have a writ for a third girl to be whipped. Now they name Elizabeth Henly."

From the hall we heard a gasp. "Oh no, oh no, oh I'm afraid I don't have the courage." Elizabeth came into the kitchen. "Oh, forgive me, Miss Crandall, I can't. Oh, why have they named me?" She turned to Miss Almira.

"Because you are from Philadelphia. And there will be others." Miss Almira tied the strings of her bonnet. "I must go and give sustenance to the girls. They will be walking across the green shortly."

"I will think of something," Miss Crandall promised. Elizabeth Henly was still sobbing softly as we left the house, too, to walk the two miles to church in Packerville.

Gloom settled over the house all the rest of that day and into Monday. On Tuesday the sheriff was expected to conduct the girls to town to be publicly whipped. The whole idea was so monstrous no one could speak of it. On Monday afternoon I volunteered to take my basket and get some supplies from Stephen Coit. Absentmindedly, Miss Crandall gave me permission and money.

I gave Stephen Coit my list over the counter, determined not to bring the matter up, yet anxious to know if he would. He did.

"Bad doings at the school, I hear," he said.

"Yes."

"My father doesn't like any of this. Just so you know."

I nodded.

"He'd take any way out, he would." Over the counter his brown eyes sought mine in a meaningful glance. What was he saying?

"But it's his job to uphold the law. You understand."

"Yes."

I was sewing in the keeping room before supper when my sister Sarah came in and sat down and spoke to me of the matter.

"I have offered to take Elizabeth Henly's whipping." Our noon dinner had been a dolorous affair, with Miss Crandall making an effort to be cheerful and encouraging the girls to eat. No one had eaten.

Somehow, I was not surprised. "I hope you know what you are about," I said.

"I do. I was the first girl at this school. I started all this."

"Have you told Mama and Daddy this?"

"When it is time for them to hear of it, they will."

"You will disgrace them."

"For standing up for what I believe in? They should be proud."

"And what about George Fayerweather?"

She turned her ahead away and said nothing. So I knew she and George had disagreed about it. They'd had a lovers' quarrel. I knew how my brother Charles would feel if Mariah offered herself to be whipped. "You heard Julia Williams, didn't you? You saw her scars."

"She believed in her cause at the time, and we believe in ours. What good is it all if you don't believe in something and aren't willing to sacrifice for it, Mary? If you have nothing to fall back on, nothing to hand down to your children, nothing to keep you going? You've got to stand for something in this life, Mary, to make it all worthwhile. You may not like me or my methods, but you will come to know that sooner or later."

I just stared at her, at her serene face, her smile, the look in her eyes. Truly, she believed all she said. And truly, what she said sounded admirable. What was wrong with me?

Just that I had this nagging little doubt that ruined everything. That Sarah was not doing what she was doing as much for her beliefs as she was for the notoriety it would give her.

But what if she did believe? And what if the notoriety only was part of it?

"You will come to the same end as Celinda. Toiling away for some white man, always marching to his tune, never listening to the little voice inside you that cries out in despair," she said, "and living your whole life a lie. In the face of that, what's one whipping? The white man's world gives us worse every day, minute by minute, lash by lash. And you'll take it, you and Celinda, the rest of your lives."

She was hurting me. So I no longer wanted to consider the problem, to give her the benefit of the doubt.

"And what of the other girls in your group? You think they believe like you do?" I asked.

My sister looked at me. "One thing you should learn, Mary Harris, if you want to be considered true grown. Sometimes good things are done for the wrong reasons. Don't ever look into a person's reasons or you'll always be disappointed. Just look at the good accomplished."

And with that she was gone.

After supper Miss Crandall left to go to Brooklyn, the county seat, which was only six miles away. She went to seek help from friends, Reverend May especially. He had become her solace.

"I shall be home in the morning. Early," she told us on leaving. "Keep heart. Not one of my girls shall feel the lash. I promise."

Then she took me aside. "No matter what happens tomorrow morning, do not let the sheriff take the girls away until I return," she said. "Promise!"

"But how could I stop him, ma'am?"

"You are friends with Stephen, are you not?"

I stared up at her. "Yes. He sells us food."

"The talk is you two are fast friends. Others buying in the store have seen it and reported to Reverend May that this is just the thing I am pushing for in town, to have Negro girls marry the white bachelors."

I felt a wave of shock, as if slapped. "It isn't that way, Miss Crandall."

"I know it, Mary. And they know it, too. But it is just the

sort of thing they like to wave under my nose, your friendship with Stephen."

I felt my lips tremble. "Do you forbid it, then?"

"Must I?"

"No, ma'am."

"Very well, then. I do not forbid it. But I ask you now, if you find it in your heart, use that friendship if you must, to protect your sisters. Do the best you can. Appeal to the sheriff. Tell him I wish to accompany my girls if they are to be whipped. That I must be there. That this is the least he can do for me, as headmistress of this school. Tell him it would be indecent to allow them to go through such an ordeal without the moral support of their teacher. Mary—" She cupped her hand under my chin and held me fast, looking steadfastly at me. "Mary, hear me now. I cannot trust my sister Almira. She is caught up in the passion of the moment. And the other girls all have their own hearts to follow. You have always been my confidante. Promise me you will do this for me, Mary."

My heart hammered inside me. What did she have planned? Could Reverend May help her?

What if he couldn't? I was terrified. But I promised.

It was full dusk as I crept out the back door after Miss Crandall's carriage had left and made my way into town. Going out alone was forbidden anymore at the school, but I was allowed out on my trips to Stephen's store because I was a town girl and people knew my family.

Still, if Miss Almira found out, I would be punished. A girl could be put out of school for disobeying the rules. I must be careful.

Stephen was just closing up the store when I got there. A single whale oil lamp glowed from within as I knocked at the front door. The street was deserted. Everyone was home at supper.

"Mary, what is it? Do you need supplies this late?" I had brought my basket in case I was caught. I would say I'd come out to get Miss Crandall some hyson-souchong tea, which she so loved and which only Stephen carried in his store.

He invited me in. I told him why I'd come. He listened solemnly, then summarized the matter. "So you want me to convince my father to wait until Miss Crandall returns on the morrow before he takes the girls away, is that it?"

"Yes, Stephen. Could you?"

"I could. For you." He smiled at me.

I blushed. His smile made me warm all over, like the Franklin stove he always kept lighted in the store.

"I don't know if he'll heed me, but I'll ask," he said.

"Thank you, Stephen. Now, if you could just give me some of Miss Crandall's favorite tea. In case I'm stopped on the street. Or Miss Almira discovers I went out."

He gave me the tea. I had forgotten to bring money. He said not to worry, bring it next time. He gave me some taffy, too, and I hurried home, his promise warm inside me.

Chapter Eighteen

———⋗◆⋖———

The next morning as I took my seat at the breakfast table, Miss Almira stood, pale of face and weak of voice.

"Girls, my sister is not yet returned from Brooklyn." And to the murmurs of dismay she held up her hand. "But we shall pray for God's guidance and strength and conduct ourselves today in accordance with His laws, the foremost of which is obedience."

With that she began to pray and everyone joined in. Part of the prayer was that we should have the courage to accept what befell us this day for the greater good of all. When she was finished and we commenced to eat, or try to eat, I spoke up.

"Miss Almira, Miss Crandall left instructions with me. She said no one should leave the house with the sheriff until she returns."

"Left instructions with you?" Miss Almira smiled.

I saw Julia Williams sitting very straight, biting her lower lip, and betimes closing her eyes. She was not eating. Her body was like a coiled spring, and I knew it would not stay quiet for long.

"Yes ma'am, that's what she instructed," I said.

"Well, she said nothing of the sort to me, and I am her sister. So I say that when the sheriff comes we will depart and obey the law. To do otherwise would make a dreadful scene."

"To do otherwise would be the only sensible thing to do," Julia put in.

"Hush, Julia. I am in charge here," Miss Almira ordered.

"In charge?" Julia said incredulously. "*They* are in charge, not you. Those who would strip young girls and whip them in public!" She stood up. "Miss Almira, if you allow this to happen this day I shall leave this school. I shall!"

"No one is whipping you, Julia," Miss Almira said sharply. "Now, sit down."

"They'll get to me, soon enough. They'll get to every one of us who isn't from the precious freedom-loving state of Connecticut. And I'll not be whipped again in my life, Miss Almira. No one will whip me again. Ever! I'll kill them first."

There was a rush of murmuring from around the table. Some of the girls voiced agreement, others dismay. "Julia!" Now Miss Almira stood. "This is a Quaker home, we do not speak of killing. Is that all Miss Crandall's teachings mean to you?"

"I'll kill them," Julia whispered savagely. Her lips were

trembling. Tears formed in her eyes. "I been whipped, not you all. I know." And with that she fled the room.

"Now, see what you have caused," Miss Almira flung at me.

I stood, steadfast as Julia. "I am only doing what Miss Crandall asked me to do. And I shall follow her wishes," I said.

At that moment one of the girls caught sight of the people who were already gathered on the green where the punishment was to be meted out. Some of the girls raced to the window to see, but Miss Almira's voice stopped them.

"Eat, girls," Miss Almira directed. "We all need our strength."

They sat back down, though no eating was accomplished. Then Mrs. Mallard came into the room, wiping her hands on her apron. "Miss Almira, Miss Sarah has a visitor, a Mr. George Fayerweather. He's in the kitchen."

"I don't wish to see him," Sarah snapped.

But in an instant George Fayerweather was in the room. He was a well-built man, being a blacksmith, and he was dressed in his smithy clothes, looking as if he'd just left his shop. "Excuse me," he apologized. "But, Miss Almira, I just can't let Miss Sarah do this thing today. Sarah!" He looked at her, then said, "You come along with me, right now. We'll go out the back door."

"George, you are embarrassing me," Sarah said. She did not look at him, she did not even stand. She pretended to be stirring her coffee.

"No woman of mine is going under the lash," George said.

Everyone waited. Mrs. Mallard stood just behind him, still

wiping her hands. All eyes were on Sarah. "I am my own woman, George," she said.

"A crazy woman is what you are," George shouted, then lowered his voice. "And for what? For this?" He gestured with his hand, taking in the whole house, the table, the girls. What meaning we were to take from the gesture we did not know. "Sarah, I can't allow it. You think I'm going to stand by and see you whipped?"

"Then I suggest you leave, George," Sarah said sweetly, "so you won't see it."

For one dreadful moment he took a step toward her chair, then he stopped. We held our breath. I wished he would drag her from the room. I wished he had never come. I wished Miss Crandall would return. I wished I could run upstairs with Julia.

Then I knew the time for wishing was past. And the time had come to act. "No one is going to whip anybody, George." I got up and went to him. I put a hand on his arm. He looked at me with such distress in his eyes that I am sure he did not know me.

"Miss Crandall has asked me not to allow the sheriff to take the girls until she returns," I said gently, "and I shall do that when he comes. And he will listen to me, I promise."

"Why should he?" George mumbled.

"Because his son is a friend of mind. And Stephen has promised he would."

"You sure about that?" George asked. There was hope in his eyes now. I felt so sorry for him, for he was surely in a predicament here. And if I were to be whipped and had a betrothed, I would want him to act the same way. Anything less would be intolerable. Sarah was a fool not to fully appreciate him.

"Yes, I'm sure. So you can stay. Or go and trust that nothing will happen," I told him.

"I have had just about enough of this!" Miss Almira got out of her chair and came over to me. "You go to your room, miss. You will be attended to later."

George stood in front of me then and faced her down. "You try and make her," he said.

"What?" Miss Almira went white in the face. She put a hand to her eyes, as if to brush away the image of him. And I don't know what all would have happened to the whole sorry mess of us then if the sheriff did not come just then. At the sound of a horse outside, several girls ran to the hall. "Oh, Miss Almira, he's here!"

All of them rushed into the hall, as if to receive callers. Sheriff Coit was alone. All watched in dreadful fascinated silence as he tethered his horse and came up the steps. "Miss Crandall in?" he asked, taking off his hat.

"My sister is not in at the present. I am acting in her stead." Miss Almira stepped forward.

If only he did not look so official, standing there holding a piece of parchment. I felt myself trembling, then I felt George's presence behind me, his gentle pressure on my elbow. I stepped forward so the sheriff could see me.

"I have a writ," he said.

Miss Almira sighed and cast her gaze at the surrounding girls. Those who called themselves the Paines were restless, hands clasped in front, standing on their toes, some hard put to keep themselves from squealing or dancing. "Read it, do," Miss Almira directed.

Sheriff Coit read it. His tone was officious and loud. It said something about Miss Crandall being in defiance of the authorities in Canterbury, how she had broken the Vagrancy Law by harboring Ann Eliza Hammond and Elizabeth Henly without first paying a security which satisfied the selectmen.

It then sentenced the girls to be publicly whipped. "Are you ready to accompany me?" the sheriff asked.

"My girls are ready," said Miss Almira. And she held out her hand, gesturing to Ann Eliza, and Sarah. "Sarah Harris is offering to take the whipping for Elizabeth Henly," she said. "Elizabeth is weakened by the strain and could not bear it. We trust this will satisfy the selectmen?"

The sheriff shrugged. "I suppose," he said.

George's grip on my elbow tightened, and I spoke up. "Wait!"

All turned to look at me. The sheriff had his gaze fastened to me now. The look on his face seemed to say, "It's about time." But instead he said, "Do we have another volunteer?"

"No." Why did my voice sound so loud, so false? "I have instructions from Miss Crandall, Sheriff."

His brown eyes were Stephen's eyes. And they were begging me to go on, not to falter. I did. "She wishes no one to leave this house until she arrives home this day." I spoke my words firm and only to him. To my relief he nodded in agreement.

"I suppose I could honor those wishes. She is a good lady," he said.

"Sheriff," Miss Almira insisted, "I am acting for my sister today."

"I'm in no hurry," he said. "As for those people out there, well, they can just wait. Or go home to attend to their business, where they should be in the first place."

"I'd rather do it now and be done with it," said Ann Eliza. My sister Sarah agreed with her.

"Seems to me what'd you'd rather do doesn't come into it here," said the sheriff. "Now, if you'll all just go inside and sit down, I'm sure we can all wait a bit for Miss Crandall."

The Paine girls let their disappointment be known. Miss Almira hushed them and sent them back into the dining room. "May I offer you some coffee, Sheriff?" Miss Almira asked.

"Don't mind if I do," he said. "Don't mind at all."

And so we waited.

The tall case clock in the hall rang the hour. Eight. Then the quarter hour, then the half. No carriage sounded in the drive. Ouside the windows on the green the crowd drew closer and we could hear their murmurings. They gathered like a flock of crows.

Inside, Miss Almira had all the girls sit down and finish their breakfast. Sheriff Coit took a chair a bit away from the table. Mrs. Mallard gave him a cup of coffee. He inquired after her husband. She said he was fine. Then the sheriff held his cup of coffee in his hand and sipped it decorously, turning down any food offered him. George Fayerweather sat in another chair a bit away from the sheriff's. I noticed that they nodded to each other and the sheriff said something about bringing his horse around soon for shodding.

The girls sat quietly, eating. All that could be heard was the sound of forks on the plates and cups set down in saucers. Miss Almira, who was seated in her sister's place at the head of the table, seemed to be meditating.

Sarah and Eliza Ann glared at me. I ate, not knowing what I was chewing. Nobody spoke. Silently I prayed that Miss Crandall would come. Where was she? She'd known the sheriff was due at eight this day. How long did she think I could hold him?

Time stretched until I thought I heard it tear, rended in pieces. Inside I was ragged, torn, too. "Mary," Miss Almira said as the clock chimed a quarter to the hour, "you may start to clear."

Breakfast was not over until nine. But I knew that since I was the only girl in the house now paying her tuition by doing such chores, Miss Almira wished to humble me. Nevertheless I stood to set myself to the task.

"How long do we wait?" Miss Almira asked the sheriff.

"I have all morning," he said.

"Haven't you any pity on these girls, being made to wait like this?"

"I always give the benefit of the doubt to everybody," he said.

"My sister can do nothing to delay this morning's grim business. What can she do?" she asked him.

"If your sister requested that I wait, I will wait," he said.

Just as I was stacking some dishes and lifting them from the table there came the sound of a carriage on the stones outside. And the raised voices from the waiting people. The girls pushed back chairs in a scramble to get up, but were stopped by Miss Almira's shrill voice. "Stop! Stay where you are! Please!"

They settled down again. I stood there, a pile of dishes in my hands, while she went to the front door. Outside we heard voices, then the door opened, and Miss Crandall came in, accompanied by Reverend May.

"Are we in time?" she asked. "Oh, you are all still here, thank goodness. Oh, Sheriff Coit, how good of you to honor my wishes!" She looked pale. Her clothes were all askew. There was an air of the frantic about her.

Sheriff Coit stood. "Do you have anything that will make me deter in the completion of my actions this day, Miss Crandall?" he asked her.

"Yes, oh yes, yes, yes. Oh, I can't speak. My breath is spent." She turned to Reverend May, who pulled a paper from his pocket and handed it to the sheriff.

"I have posted bond," the good reverend said. "There is the receipt. As you can see, it covers all the girls in the school and has been approved by several prominent men in the area. It ought to protect Canterbury from any damage done by these pupils."

Sheriff Coit read the paper, nodded, and pocketed it. Then he turned to us all. "Good day, ladies," he said. "It has been pleasant spending this time with you. Miss Almira, you have been most accommodating. Miss Crandall, I have satisfied my obligations."

And with that he took his leave.

Immediately there was a ruckus. Girls gathered around Miss Crandall, hugging and kissing her. Then they sat again at the table and Mrs. Mallard brought in breakfast for Reverend May and Miss Crandall, who took off her bonnet and proceeded to tell how they'd rushed here hoping to be on time, of her fears for her girls.

Ann Eliza and Sarah asked to be excused. Sarah walked right past George, who was standing quietly in the background waiting to speak with her. But he reached out and grabbed her arm and drew her toward him. She was so drained, she just melted into his arms. Then she pulled away and he watched her go up the stairs after Ann Eliza. Some of the Paines went with them.

"Thank you," Miss Crandall said to me, as she smiled across the table. "I don't know what I would have done without you this morning, Mary."

Miss Almira left the room, glaring at me as she did so. And I had a terrible fear, deep in my bones, that I would pay for this morning. "Julia became very agitated," I said. "She's upstairs."

"I was afraid that would happen. I'll speak with her later."

But just then Julia came down the stairs, dragging her portmanteau. It bumped on each step, and George Fayerweather stepped forward to help her with it.

She thanked him and came into the dining room. "I'm leaving, Miss Crandall," she said. She was dressed in her best Sabbath-day clothes. "I want to thank you for everything you have done for me."

Everyone stared. Miss Crandall was so taken aback she could scarce speak. Then she did. "It's all over, Julia. Reverend May has posted bond, so no girls will have to be whipped. Ever."

"I'm sorry, Miss Crandall, but I don't trust that. And I can't stay in a place where girls gladly offer themselves up to the lash. Something is wrong here, ma'am. I don't know what. But I don't aim to stay around and find out. Now all I need is a ride to town, to the store where I can get the stage. I have money."

"I'll take you, Miss Williams, if you don't mind riding in a blacksmith's wagon." George Fayerweather stepped forward.

"I'd admire to, sir."

She said her good-byes. I made no attempt to stop her. In the hall she hugged me fiercely.

"Don't you forget now. 'Looking back only costs an eye. Not looking at all makes you blind.' I'll write." Then she went through the kitchen and out the back door with George.

Chapter Nineteen

———⟫•◇•⟪———

"That girl," Mrs. Mallard said, "that girl seems to be the only one with sense in this place." No sooner did she say it than we heard the thumping start in front of the house.

First there were one, two, three thumps. Mrs. Mallard and I looked at each other, then both ran across the hall and into the dining room. I felt Mrs. Mallard's hand on my arm, detaining me, but I broke loose and ran to the windows where the others were looking out.

Then came the horrible smashing sound, the shock of which set us screaming. I was mindful of several things happening at once. Of Miss Crandall with her hand in front of her mouth. Of Reverend May standing and forming his lips to tell the girls to stay away from the window and of myself feeling something whiz by, grazing the side of my head, then landing on the floor. For a moment I couldn't reason. It was as if the world exploded. Then I saw something follow the object and hit the organdy curtain on the window, press the curtain back against the window frame, break, and ooze a yellow liquid all over the curtain.

An egg. I laughed. "It's only an egg," I said. "How could an egg break the window?"

Then I felt Reverend May's hands on my shoulders guiding me away, speaking gently, asking how badly I was hurt. I sat on a chair on the far end of the room, and put my hand to my temple. It came away smeared with blood. "I've been hit with the egg," I said dully.

Miss Crandall was there in minute with a cold wet rag. "You were hit with a rock. It came through the window. Put your head back. Rest."

I did so. She held the rag to my head until the bleeding stopped, then bandaged it. The other girls milled about, stepping delicately around the shards of glass that lay about, glinting obscenely in the April sunlight.

Miss Almira and the Paines came down to see what had happened, and Miss Crandall ushered everyone out of the room. There were more thumpings, more eggs. Some came through the broken window and plopped onto the wood floor. I gazed in fascination at them. Never had I seen an egg break anywhere but in a pan or a bowl.

Then Reverend May, bearing his brass-headed cane, strode into the front hall, opened the door, and bellowed out, "For shame! For shame, you ruffians, besieging an innocent good woman and her students!"

"We came to see a whipping!" came the reply floating on

the innocent April air. "And we're not leaving until we've had some excitement!"

"You'll get more excitement than you bargained for if I come out there! Disperse now, I say! In the name of decency! Disperse immediately or I'll bring the sheriff back!"

Silence then. I looked up to see Mrs. Mallard handing me a cup of water. "You're shaking," she said.

I drank the water, minding my hand, which could scarcely hold the cup, saying nothing, but watching closely as Miss Crandall picked up the rock, set it on the mantel, and said from henceforth it would stay there.

Mariah stepped on a stool and started to take down the curtain with egg on it. "No," Miss Crandall said. "Leave it. I want it to hang there to show people what we are enduring here."

"It will smell," Mariah said.

"Some things smell worse, Mariah. Leave it."

Mariah left it. From somewhere abovestairs I heard a girl crying.

The glass was cleaned up, Reverend May left promising to send a man to repair the window, and the girls were sent to their studies, although I was told to spend the day quietly reading. I sat in the front parlor in the April sun, protesting the warm rug put around me, my eyes on my book but not able to absorb the words. Mrs. Mallard had made me a cup of special tea to becalm me.

After quietude was restored one sound persisted. The girl

crying. I heard Miss Almira and Miss Crandall upstairs with her, then after a while the crying stopped and Miss Almira came back down. "I must send someone for Dr. Harris across the green. Elizabeth Henly is feverish and has an aching head."

"I'll go, Miss Crandall."

"No, Mary. You're hurt."

"I'd be obliged for some fresh air," I said.

She relented. "Take a shawl. The green is empty now. Come directly back. And tell him we need him."

The day had turned springlike with that special something in the air that makes you remember what you missed all winter, although you could not put a name to it. The grass on the green was already bright in color, I saw at least three robins, and it seemed as if nothing under heaven could go bad on such a day in the Lord's own sunlight.

My spirits lifted, walking. We had come through a bad time, was all. We had friends, people who would help us. Then I thought, What a fool I am. There will be evil and darkness on the brightest day outside the very doors of heaven itself.

I stood on the front portico of Dr. Harris's house in God's good sunlight and knocked on the door. A mousy woman in plain black with white apron went to fetch him and give him my message. Now she was back. I waited to be invited in. I peered into the inviting richness of the center hallway beyond her, at heavy walnut wainscoting, portraits framed in dull gold, rich carpeting.

"The doctor said he can't come."

"I beg your pardon?"

"Can't come. Are you simple, child? I thought the girls she had in that house were so bright. He can't come. He says send for somebody else."

"But we have sickness. Isn't that what doctors are for?"

"Don't be sassy! Don't get above yourself! That's what they all say, that soon you'll all be above yourselves. And they're right. Get someone else!"

"Who?"

"How do I know? The doctor says she should get that brother of hers. That he saw him in town just yesterday. Seems to me that if her own brother's a physician, she shouldn't come begging. Now go, girl, and tell her."

The ornate carved door closed in my face. I stood stunned on the portico for a moment, looking across the bright green under trees lacy with spring buds. A farce, I thought. How can it be spring? How can there be hope when people are so evil?

She hadn't even asked about the bandage on my head. I started home, feeling eyes on my back. I just know that mousy woman was watching me and feeling gratified.

Miss Crandall's brother Mr. Reuben was sent for. He was staying at their father's farm, which was not far away. Miss Crandall said nothing at my report that Dr. Harris would not come, except, "We will remember him this evening at prayers." She took every opportunity to try to teach us her

Quaker ways, but none of the girls paid mind as far as I knew. I know I didn't. I was all for pelting Dr. Harris's house with some eggs myself.

"No dead cat this time, sister?" Mr. Reuben asked Miss Crandall when he came in with his father. He kissed her and gave her some newspapers. "As you can see the news of the girls being whipped has been carried all over the Northeast." Then Miss Almira took him upstairs.

Miss Crandall gave a cry of surprise and spread the papers out on the dining room table.

"The press is with thee, daughter," Mr. Pardon said. "Thee cannot fail."

I fetched him a cup of tea. He smiled down at me. "Is this the Harris child, then?"

"Yes, and she saved the day for us. She herself persuaded the sheriff to wait until I got here with Reverend May, else the girls would have been whipped," Miss Crandall said.

"And for her trouble she has gotten hit in the head." Mr. Pardon smiled. He was really not a handsome man, but when he smiled I thought I heard angels singing. "Thee best have Reuben look at her, too," he advised. "Go and sit down, child. Thee looks peaked."

He led me to a chair and sat me down himself and covered me with a blanket. What a dear man he is, I thought. His hands were callused from farming, yet they were gentle as my mama's. Something otherworldly emanated from him. I felt it soothing me.

He went back across the room then to accept a second cup of tea from his daughter, stood sipping it and examining the broken window. "A bad business," he said. "And I fear it will get worse before it gets better."

"I think we've seen the worst of it, Pa."

"They have threatened me," he told her. "They have told me they will tear down my house if I do not stop attending thee with food and water."

"Oh, the bounders!" Miss Crandall said, then caught herself, seeing me watching and minding how un-Quakerlike it was. "Pa, thee mustn't come, then."

"What?" Pardon glowered. "I'd like to see them stop me, daughter. It's something I'd like to see."

While this exchange was going I found myself trembling, and I knew the morning had caught up with me. There was danger, all around, I decided. Then I decided I was becoming like Julia, looking for the overseer with his whip. Of a sudden I longed to go home. Perhaps Miss Crandall would let me go. I would ask her when Mr. Reuben and Mr. Pardon left.

I leaned my head back and closed my eyes. In a moment I felt snatches of sleep claiming me even as I heard Miss Crandall and Mr. Pardon tiptoe from the room. I don't recollect how long I dozed, but soon I felt a gentle touch on my forehead. I opened my eyes.

Mr. Reuben stood over me. "Well, and so you've had a bad morning, have you?" he asked.

I shrank from him. He frightened me.

"May I remove the bandage and see to your wound?"

I nodded yes. He did so, carefully. Then he poked around in his doctor's bag and drew out some remedies and poked and dabbed at my cut. All the while he asked me how I had liked Boston, if I had seen Dr. Harris at all, and did I know he had studied with Dr. Harris at one time? I answered his questions directly, gaining confidence minute by minute, scarce aware while he rewrapped my head, fished into his bag, drew out a tablet, and gave it to me with some water.

I swallowed it, making a face. Again he reached into his bag, took a peppermint out and gave it to me.

Then he got serious. "You like my sister, don't you?" he asked.

I said yes, I did.

"Does she speak well of me?"

"She thinks you're too bossy."

He smiled. "Don't you consider your brother Charles too bossy?"

"You know Charles?"

"I know about your whole family. Especially you. Miss Prudence has told me what a faithful friend you are to her. And what a good companion. I like to think my headstrong sister has good companions and faithful friends. Will you do something for me?"

"I won't spy on her for you," I said firmly.

He smiled again. "I wouldn't ask such of you."

"What would you ask, then? And why should I do it?"

"My, you all have spirit around here, don't you? Even that girl who left, what was her name?"

"Julia Williams. She left because she was once whipped and she said she'd never be whipped again and nobody could convince her it wouldn't come to that."

"I don't blame her one bit. But look here, back to why it would be in your interest to help me. Let's say because my brother and I both know the mill owners where your sister works in Massachusetts. And my brother Hezekiah can put in a good word for her if it is ever needed."

I met his eyes. He didn't blink. So he, too, knew about Celinda's passing as white. "What do you want me to do for you? I won't try to convince her to give up the school, either."

"I would ask you to stay by her side in the days ahead. No matter what happens. She trusts you and I would ask you to honor that trust like you did this morning. I have to go back home to Peekskill, but I shall be back. If things get bad around here I would ask you to send for my father. And stay with her, always. Would you do that?"

"The other day you tried to tell her she must close the school. You wanted Miss Almira to leave. What changed your mind?"

He smiled. Like his father, there was a sweetness to him. "Anyone who is willing to endure what my sister, and you girls, are going through here deserves backing. I have decided to back her. But I need your help. Will you?"

I said yes, I would. He left some tablets for me to take that night. I fell asleep in the chair and didn't wake until much later. When I did, it was to a knocking on the front door. In the hallway Miss Prudence was speaking to the postman who had delivered some packages. Gifts.

I helped open them. There was a lovely bible, bound in rich leather with a note that said something about Miss Crandall's "Christian courage." There were two bound volumes of *Cruden's Concordance*, and, carefully wrapped, two Staffordshire plates decorated with pictures of Negro people around the border. These came from some abolitionist ladies in Boston.

Miss Crandall put the plates on the dining room mantel. Right next to the rock that had hit my head.

Chapter Twenty

Two days later I got my chance to keep my promise to Mr. Reuben. Two men knocked on the green front door while we were at our noon meal. Mrs. Mallard answered the knock. Because I was helping her in the kitchen, I went with her.

One said he was Selectman Ashael Bacon. The other identified himself as Selectman Ebenezer Sanger. And after they told the purpose of their visit, I knew who they really were. Overseers. Still pursuing us. Julia would have known them before they opened their mouths.

"Is Miss Crandall in?" the one who called himself Selectman Bacon asked.

I was sent to fetch her. And I stood behind her when Selectman Bacon asked: "Are you harboring students from abroad?"

"Gentleman, you know I have girls from several states here," Miss Crandall told them.

Then she invited them in, and ushered them into the

dining room. There she introduced them to all the girls, one by one. And, one by one the girls stood and curtsied and answered questions about where they hailed from.

The selectmen thanked Miss Crandall and left.

The next day, in the evening, Deputy Sheriff George Cady knocked on the door. Once again I accompanied Mrs. Mallard.

He stood there with his hat in his hands. "I apologize for the disturbance."

"Is there going to be a disturbance?" Mrs. Mallard asked.

"I'm afraid so. Are the two Misses Crandall in?"

Again I was sent to fetch them. They came with a rustling of skirts. Deputy Sheriff Cady gave a small bow and took a paper out of his pocket. A thrill of dread went through me. "Miss Prudence Crandall and Miss Hannah Almira Crandall?" he asked.

"I'm called Almira," she said.

"Yes, miss. I have have here an order for both your arrests."

Gasps. I am afraid that mine was the loudest, more like a moan. Miss Crandall was stoic.

"On what charges, sir?" she asked.

"For going against the Black Law. The charge has been brought by Nehemiah Ensworth. You are both to accompany me immediately to the house of Selectman Bacon for arraignment."

"Get our cloaks, please, Mary," Miss Crandall said.

I was trembling. She was going. My hands shook as I handed them their cloaks.

Arraignment. What did it mean? Was it as bad as whipping? She smiled down at me. "Go and ask Mrs. Mallard if she will stay the night. Tell Sarah and Mariah to close up the house as usual. And tell everyone not to worry. We'll be fine. But if we don't come back tonight, tomorrow send for Mr. Hezekiah and my father. They'll know what to do."

It was coming on to dusk as they went outside. I watched as the deputy sheriff helped them into his chaise. Of a sudden the hallway was filled with girls. "They've been arrested," I said, "and taken away. Oh, Mrs. Mallard, can you stay the night?"

They sent Miss Almira home, delivered her home in a chaise driven by the deputy sheriff.

He tipped his hat as he drove away and Miss Almira stood there like a disgruntled kitten, glowering after him. "They've set bail for my sister," she said. "A hundred and fifty dollars. Of course she doesn't have it. Justice of the Peace Rufus Adams sent for Reverend May. They're all waiting for him."

"Will they let her come home tonight?" Mariah asked.

"Likely. But it'll be midnight, I wager." She lifted her skirts and stamped into the house. "Oh, I hate that Nehemiah Ensworth. Don't you recollect his daughter Frances? She was one of Miss Crandall's white students who was put out. I suppose this is his way of getting even!"

"Why did they let you go?" Mrs. Mallard asked.

Miss Almira tossed her head. "Because I'm a minor! Wait until my brothers and father hear of this. Just wait!" And she flounced up the stairs.

Miss Crandall did come home that night. Lying in my bed I heard her come in. I got up and crept down to the second floor where the girls had all come from their beds, too, to greet her.

"I'm home to sleep," she said, "and to pack. Tomorrow I go to jail."

There were cries of indignation, even some wails. "Didn't Reverend May post bond?" Mariah asked.

"He is too good a friend of mine to do so, for it would relieve all those eminent gentlemen of their embarrassment. That's what I told them. They must put me in jail, I said. I go tomorrow to Brooklyn. Sheriff Coit will come and fetch me. Go to bed, all of you now. School will go on as usual tomorrow. We cannot have our routine interrupted." Then she saw me, huddling in the background. "Mary, come help me pack, will you dear?"

In the bedroom, once the door was closed, she held me for a moment. "Senator Pearl, whose daughter was put out of the school, was head of the committee that drew up the Black Law just passed by the Connecticut General Assembly," she told me. "Fetch my gray wool dress. It may be chilly in prison."

I went to the clothes press and got it out.

"And Mr. Judson drove to my father's farm to warn him that

every time he visits this school he will be fined a hundred dollars. My dear father! Oh, Mary, I can stand anything they do I can to me, but to hurt such a good man as my father!" She started to cry.

"Miss Crandall, I must go with you," I said.

She stopped midstep. "Go with me? To jail?" Her delicate eyebrows rose with the impossibility of it, then settled again as a gleam came into her eyes. "And so you shall. Pack your things for overnight. In the morning when we leave, I shall send a note to your parents."

I could scarce believe she'd said yes. And for a moment I was terror struck. We were going to jail! She was taking me with her! I ran to pack. Am I getting like the other girls, I asked myself, like the Paines? I thought of Julia. What would she say? Am I betraying Julia? Or doing right by keeping my promise to Mr. Reuben?

The day was as bright and as beautiful a one as spring could offer. One thought of going on a picnic, on a visit to friends. One could not believe one was going to jail.

The girls were all crowded around the sheriff's carriage. There were kisses and hugs. I heard a gasp from Sarah. "You're taking Mary?"

"I need a friend," Miss Crandall said.

"I should be going," Miss Almira snapped. "If I'm not allowed because I'm a minor, why is she?"

"I've sent a note to her parents to be at the jail to give

permission," Miss Crandall told her.

"You could have given permission for me!" Miss Almira glared at me and I felt the heat of her hatred. Then Miss Crandall pulled her aside. I saw her scolding gently. Then I heard the words, "nigra servant, and it isn't the same." I flushed. Miss Almira put her nose up in the air and walked off, satisfied.

The girls pressed things to us. A basket of food, napkins, a bible, a book, handkerchiefs. Even a blanket. They were too struck numb to object to my going. Some of them were crying as we drove off. As we settled in the carriage, Miss Crandall pressed my hand and smiled at me.

"Don't be frightened," she said, "No one will harm us. Oh, look, there are some citizens who support us now."

I looked. The road was lined with maple trees and for at least a mile, as it sloped from Canterbury to Brooklyn, it was lined with people. They waved and shouted encouragement to us. Some threw flowers.

At the Brooklyn jail there was another crowd. Waiting for us. They turned curious faces as we arrived. The men took off their hats. "What is this?" Miss Crandall asked.

I looked desperately through the crowd, and was comforted and saddened at the same time to see Stephen Coit. I wanted to cry then, to jump down from the carriage and run to him, a true friend. It was frightening, being stared at. And more frightening seeing the jail, a low frame building with a rickety porch.

What am I doing here, I asked myself. How did all this come to be?

Reverend May was there and he came over to help us down from the chaise. "If you have changed your mind, I will post bail for you now," he whispered. "This is no place for a lady. And they intend to put you in the cell once occupied by Oliver Watkins."

"My only fear is that they will not put me in jail," she told him.

This pronouncement made me sick and for a moment I felt dizzy. Faces swayed in front of me. The name Oliver Watkins swirled in my brain. I knew who he was. He had strangled his wife and was hanged two years ago. Now we were to be put in his cell?

Sheriff Coit ushered us through the crowd.

"Let the woman go! Let the woman go!" the crowd started to chant softly. But Sheriff Coit and Reverend May paid no mind. Then I heard a voice.

"Courage, Mary." Soft as the wind, yet distinct.

I looked up. And there in the front of the line of people was Stephen Coit. He had flowers in his hand, wildflowers. He stepped forward and handed a bunch to Miss Crandall. And another to me. I inhaled their sweet fragrance, murmured my thanks, and was led along by the sheriff.

We were met at the door by the jailer, Mr. Tyler. "Are you ready to be incarcerated, Miss Crandall?" he asked.

"I am."

"Do you understand that you must stay a full night? With no companionship?"

"I do. But I have brought my companion. She will stay with me."

He looked at me. "She is a minor. I will not jail her."

"She is my helpmate," Miss Crandall said. She would not use the words "nigra servant" in front of me.

"I cannot put her inside without permission of her parents."

At that moment the wagon with Mama and Daddy came up the road and everyone turned to look. Daddy got down and came through the crowd, right to me. "Daughter." And he hugged me, much in the same way he used to hug Sarah. Then he looked at the sheriff. "What is it you need from me, sir? My permission to allow my daughter to accompany Miss Crandall? She has my permission."

Mr. Tyler made him sign a paper. That being done, Daddy stepped away so Mr. Tyler and Sheriff Coit could do their duty. Sheriff Coit walked off a bit to confer with a few men who looked important, then came back. Then one of the men who looked pious and solemn came over to Reverend May. "It would be a damn shame and an eternal disgrace to put this woman in that wife murderer's cell," he said.

Reverend May agreed. "If you would drop the charges we could all go home," he said.

So then, this must be Mr. Ensworth, whose daughter Frances had gone to our school.

"But we are not her friends," Mr. Ensworth said. "And we

don't want any more nigras coming among us. You are the one who should prevent this, sir. You should post bail. You are deserting her in her hour of need."

"She knows we have not deserted her," Reverend May replied.

Mr. Ensworth stepped back and Mr. Tyler escorted us inside. After the bright sunlight outside I could scarce see at first. I did see bars on the small windows, and the place smelled musty and damp. Mr. Tyler led us to our cell, and I was surprised to see freshly whitewashed walls and two beds. On them was piled fresh bedding.

"Sent by friends," Mr. Tyler said.

Miss Crandall thanked him and he left. The door clanged shut. I stood looking at her. She smiled and lighted a small candle on a nearby table. "I have brought books," she said, and she drew them out of her basket. "We can read and the time will go swiftly." She took off her bonnet and set it aside.

I felt near tears. Outside I could hear the people chanting softly, "Let the woman go, let the woman go."

"You are good to stay by me, Mary," she said. "I shall not forget this."

We stayed one day. We ate the food in the hamper, we read, we talked, and we prayed. She told me about her family, how the first Crandall to arrive in America was John in 1635.

"He was an Anabaptist," she said. "He was banished from Massachusetts with Roger Williams. To Rhode Island, which was then a wilderness. He was an outcast, but he prospered and did well."

She told me how her mother and father had not always been Quakers. "At their wedding my mother wore black satin. An Empire-style dress, trimmed with red and yellow satin. And a red cloak. They became Quakers years after their marriage."

I was with her through it all. In no records will anyone find my name, however, because Mr. Tyler did not mark me down in his books. I was her colored servant girl, and as such was not a citizen. The Black Law just passed by the General Assembly said so.

We slept on the clean bedding provided by her father. During the night a hooty owl called outside my window. The last thing Miss Crandall said to me that night was "You can tell your grandchildren, Mary, how you suffered the lot of an outcast for your beliefs."

But I was not suffering, I minded. We'd had a scrumptious supper, we'd kept each other company, the bedding smelled of lavender, and I knew friends and family anxiously awaited my release. That some even wished they were in here in my stead.

We got out the next day. Friends of hers, the family of Henry Benson, provided bail.

The *Windham County Advertiser* said the whole business was "a sham, a farce, it was trickery at its worst. She has sought publicity by ridiculously spending a night in prison without the smallest necessity of it," they wrote. "She has stepped out of the hallowed precincts of female propriety and now stands on common ground and must expect common treatment."

Another said she was the instrument of Mr. Garrison.

But jail did the trick. Many more newspapers favored her. So did the common people. Mail came now from Canada, from Europe. That summer all kinds of important personages visited our school. We were required to perform for them. Miss Almira coached the younger girls to recite. She made me be a part of it. We were dressed in white. I was embarrassed, but dared not object.

One of these visitors was Mr. Garrison. Another Mr. Arthur Tappan, a wealthy man who had encouraged Miss Crandall. Every time one of these important visitors was rumored to be coming, a group of rowdy boys would greet the stagecoach on the town limits and run after it through town, chanting and throwing things, even shooting off rifles in the air. Then, at some signal the bells of the Congregational Church would chime loudly for hours, while the visitors took tea inside.

We went on. Summer set itself over the land. People stayed out of the heat. I learned how to play the pianoforte, how to make a Marlborough pie, how to do a French seam, to sit and walk like a lady, how to keep conversation going at the table without touching on topics to offend anyone. I learned the principles of our government. I learned ciphering and geography and geometry. I read as much as I wanted to and nobody stopped me.

One day I visited Stephen Coit at the store. I brought him

a Marlborough pie for his friendship. He thanked me. "Visitors who come here say they hear the mood inside is cheerful and intimate. That love binds everyone together."

We laughed over that. "Miss Almira hates me," I told him. "My sister Sarah and I scarce speak anymore. She belongs to the Paines. And Miss Crandall thinks the more of her for having the strength of her convictions. The Paines dress all in black. If lessons are held outside under the maple trees, they look like crows."

"Gossip has it that Mr. Tappan had offered to be Reverend May's banker, and had instructed the good reverend to spare no expense for Miss Crandall, but to hire the best legal counsel he can get," he said.

"For what?" I asked.

He raised his eyebrows. "Why for Miss Crandall's trial. Hasn't she told her students? She goes on trial soon for going against the Black Law."

Chapter Twenty-one

At first I was disappointed at not being in the papers or on the official records for going to jail with Miss Crandall. It was Stephen who told me what the advantages were.

"Don't you see?" he said one day in the store. "If they don't regard you as anybody important enough to keep a record of, you can effect change and never be blamed for it."

"How?" I asked.

"In any way you wish, when the right moment comes, Mary," he explained. "If they don't count you as a person, a citizen, then they won't be looking at you when something important is done to go against their wishes."

"I don't know what I could ever do of importance," I said.

He gave me that look of his, as if I should know, as if words were not necessary between us. "When the time comes, you will know it, Mary. If you are willing to be counted on. Are you?"

I said yes. And in the next moment wondered just what it was I had agreed to, what promise I had entered into. Because

I knew I had done both, without realizing.

I went on with my studies, taking a back seat in the goings on at the seminary. My spirit was cast down, though, because since I'd been to jail, my sister Sarah was snubbing me. The pain of it was deep. Sarah and I hadn't always gotten on, but she was my older sister. I missed her, but did not press myself upon her. In time, I told myself, she would come around.

The Paines, on the other hand, were in their season of importance. Once Miss Crandall told us about the trial, they seemed to stay even more to themselves, whispering and plotting, about what was anybody's guess. The trial was to begin in late August in Brooklyn. They begged to be allowed to go to court wearing their black costumes. Miss Crandall said no court, no. They begged to be allowed to learn about the three men Reverend May had hired to defend her, William Ellsworth, Calvin Goddard, and Henry Strong. Miss Crandall said yes to that.

"But the school must go on and your studies not interrupted. If they are, those who fight us will have achieved their purpose."

So when the trial started in late August, the girls stayed home. Mariah and Sarah taught classes. Miss Almira was finally able to help. She was full of self-importance, quick to scold and even quicker to punish.

Daily we received personal bulletins from Miss Crandall, who wrote us a brief letter and sent it home every night, though she stayed with her friends the Bensons in Brooklyn.

Miss Almira read the letter at supper, and put special emphasis on the name *Benson*. Anyone who had misbehaved in class that day she maliciously sent from the room so they could not hear it.

The courtroom was crowded, Miss Crandall wrote. Judge Eaton had a spirit of hostility toward her. He allowed the prosecution lawyers to address her as "Prudy."

They might summon one or two girls as witnesses, to ask them what was taught in the school. If they did, her lawyers said we had the right to refuse to answer on the grounds that we might incriminate ourselves.

The girls in the Paines became so excited at the reading of this letter they could scarce eat. They hoped and prayed to be summoned to court. A few were, Mary Elizabeth Wiles, Ann Peterson, Catherine Ann Weldon, and Ann Eliza Hammond. They were beside themselves with importance. And when they returned they were immediately surrounded by the rest of the Paines, enfolded and questioned and whispered at and to. And they would not tell the rest of us what had happened.

Except for the man in the blue cravat.

Those who had been summoned to court went on separate days. And upon returning at night each of them talked about the man in the blue cravat at supper.

"He is six feet two," said Mary Wiles.

"He is a Baptist preacher," said Ann Eliza Hammond.

"He is a widower," reported Catherine Ann Weldon.

And they would giggle amongst themselves at their end of the table, the Paines.

"Come, include the rest of the girls in your report," admonished Miss Almira. "It isn't polite to whisper."

So Catherine Ann spoke up then. "He spoke to me today. And you will never guess what he said. He said that he intended to marry Miss Crandall."

Bursts of giggles then and Miss Almira had to rap on the table with her fork. "Girls, girls, this is gossip. And you know how Miss Crandall feels about gossip. It is most unseemly."

A letter came from Celinda:

> *Dear Mary:*
>
> *I am sorry I have not written in so long, but I have been so busy with my work and my studies that I am too tired at night to do anything. And I must, of course, keep up my correspondence with Mama and Daddy.*
>
> *Yes, I said studies. For the reading group I belong to has been reading novels, something I never did at home, things I never knew existed. We have read Richardson, Fielding, and Scott. And we discuss them! I cannot tell you how contented such guilty pleasures make me feel. We belong to a circulating library.*
>
> *Mama wrote to me about your confinement overnight in jail! Dear sister! How brave of you! But why did you not write and tell me of it? Are you not proud?*
>
> *I have become more involved in a fight, too, though I did*

not wish to be. It seems that the owners of the mill want to cut our wages and increase our work day by half an hour so that we would be starting earlier in the morning. Some of the girls can scarce get up so early now. And the older ones in our house have come to calling it oppression.

I tell you honestly, sister, when the word was first used in connection with white girls of good standing I was shocked. How could white people be oppressed, you might ask. Even as I did before I came here. But I see it now, before my eyes. And I am, indeed, part of it.

Do you recollect how Charles and Mariah read The Liberator and spoke of oppression of our Southern brothers and sisters? Well, it goes on here in great plenty. Some of the girls I work with are sick with what we call the "mill cough," yet if they take so much as a day off from their jobs they lose pay. Others are worn to death by taking on too much work so they can earn extra wages, and for the most part we are all slaves to the people who run and own the mill.

I never saw young women work so hard, not even any house servants we knew at home. Yet the managers and agents are not happy and wish to make us now work harder and reduce our pay. Some of the older girls who have been here a while propose a march at night to show our displeasure. I opened my mouth and said why not do it during the day, after the noon meal, instead of returning to work? That would set the mill production back and they would feel the loss.

Well, of course I had to go and open my mouth, so now I am part of the planning of it. And though I am frightened, I know it is the right thing to do. For myself and other girls who follow. Think, Mary. One of them might be you. I would hate to bring you up here right now with such threatening conditions. And so I too now fight for a cause.

It seems that the times, dear sister, produce causes all around. If not one, than another needs our attention. All we can do is trust in God that he will see us through. Write to me.

Your loving sister, Celinda.

When *The Hartford Courant* reported that the students who had appeared in court were "intelligent, well-mannered, and tastefully dressed," the Paines were unfit to live with. The story went on to say that they had "better claims to grace and beauty than most of the belles and matrons in the district."

And it mentioned their names.

There was so much boasting and hilarity over that that Miss Almira had to deliver a special sermon about humility and demand silence at supper until Miss Crandall returned.

She returned at the end of the week. The jury could not reach an opinion. Seven voted for conviction and five for acquittal. The judge said the case must be continued next term in December.

She returned with the man in the blue cravat. His name was Calvin Philleo. He held her by the arm. A young girl was with them, tall and gangly with a sallow complexion. We watched as Miss Crandall and Mr. Philleo came up the walk, speaking as if they'd known each other forever. We stared and stepped back, parting ranks like the waters parted for Moses. We had never seen Miss Crandall with a man and could not imagine how she knew how to behave with one.

"I heard that he was put out of a church in Suffield," said Ann Eliza Hammond.

"I heard that he is so desperate to find a wife that he's even advertised for one," said Ann Weldon.

"Girls, hush!" said Miss Almira. "Let us give this man the benefit of the doubt!" But when I looked I saw she had her handkerchief up to her face. And that she was crying.

The girl's name was Elizabeth. She was fourteen and she sat at the kitchen table sipping tea as Mrs. Mallard prepared supper and Mariah and I helped. Roast duckling, stuffed squash, potatoes, cabbage, beets. It was a celebration supper. I had made my Marlborough pie.

"And so, where do you go to school, Elizabeth?" Mariah asked her.

"I go to a day school in Rhode Island. With white girls," she said.

Mariah raised an eyebrow and gave me a quick look. I thought she was about to say something when she saw Mr. Pardon pulling up outside in his wagon with supplies. She excused herself and went out to greet him.

"How long will you and your father be visiting our town, then?" I asked.

"Oh," she waved a hand languidly, "we never intended to come at all. We were on the Suffield stagecoach on the return journey from visiting my brother at school when my father heard about Miss Crandall's trial and decided to attend it. He's been looking for a wife, you know. Preferably a woman with property and standing."

Mrs. Mallard stopped slicing her potatoes. "Looking for a wife, is he?" she asked.

"Oh yes," the girl said. "He's been looking for some time."

And at that moment Mr. Pardon came into the kitchen with Mariah, lugging his vegetables. Mariah introduced him. She offered him some refreshment. He sat down at the table and started telling us about how the people were turning against Andrew Judson and others accusing Miss Crandall. "His harshness toward my daughter turned the jury against him," Mr. Pardon said.

I saw Elizabeth eyeing him with disdain, and soon she excused herself and got up and left the room.

Chapter Twenty-two

"Miss Crandall?"

"Yes, Mary?"

I stood in the doorway of her room with a tray of tea and some corn bread. It was raining and she was crying. The girls were whispering about it and Mariah had sent me up with the tray. Philleo and his daughter had left late the night before, after our supper of roast duckling. By the time she had left, every girl in the house hated Elizabeth Philleo. She had poked into every corner, asked every rude question, and swished her skirts disdainfully at us.

"Don't think I'm going to live in a house with nigra girls," she had said. I hadn't heard her say it, Mariah did.

"She's trouble, that one," Mariah had told me. "And I think so is he. You know what the daughter told me? That her father thinks this school is a poor financial investment that will come to nothing and absorb all Miss Crandall's funds. Even while he applauds Miss Crandall's efforts. And she bragged about the fact that one woman, a milliner, had to throw her father out of his shop when he would not leave her be. She calls him dashing. I call him a womanizer!"

"Miss Crandall I've brought tea. You didn't eat breakfast." It was midmorning, Saturday. I knew she'd be doing correspondence. She dabbed at her eyes with a handkerchief and directed me to come in.

I served the tea. Her hand trembled when she raised the cup to her lips. I waited to be dismissed, but she said nothing, so I lingered. "You're good to me, Mary," she said.

I breathed easier. "Do you have a cold?" I asked.

"Yes, the worst kind, Mary. A cold in my heart."

"Has your friend gone back to Rhode Island then?"

"I've sent him back," she said.

I waited. There would be more, I was sure of it. There was.

"I've heard all the rumors, Mary. Don't think I haven't. Rumors that bespeak ill of him. I do not believe them for a minute, mind you."

"Then why are you crying?" I asked.

"Because he knows I have heard the rumors. Even from the mouth of his own daughter, who does not want him to marry again. I cry because I have waited for him to dispel those rumors. He has not done so. So I have sent him away."

I thought for a moment. "Does he know you are waiting for him to speak?"

"I did not say this, Mary. How could I? No, it must come from him, not because I ask it of him. And so this is why I cry. Oh dear, I sin from weakness. I must pray, Mary. Go now, please, I must be alone. And don't tell anyone of this conversation, please."

Before I left, she kissed me. I left with a special warmth inside me. It was the last moment of real closeness between us.

It is difficult to think that some people come into our lives, even for just one day, create chaos, and then in the end serve to give us a turn of mind which we never would have arrived at had they not come.

It is pride to think they were sent just for us. But what else can I think of Mr. Frederick Olney?

I was at Stephen's store when I first met Mr. Olney. It was late September and we were talking of the double wedding of my sister Sarah and George Fayerweather and Mariah and my brother Charles in November.

"Some celebration. Good times at the seminary for a change," Stephen said. "Tell Miss Crandall she can expect a basket of my best delicacies for the occasion." I thanked him and he eyed me carefully. "Is that Mr. Philleo still coming around?"

"He's gone back to his church in Rhode Island for a while."

Just then the stagecoach rumbled up and one passenger got out, a Negro man with lots of bundles, dressed in everyday clothing, and wearing spectacles. He came directly into the store, looked around, and sniffed. "I smell coffee," he said.

"Frederick! Good to see you!" Stephen came out from behind the counter and shook the man's hand vigorously as he struggled to set his bundles down. "Did you have a good trip?"

"If you don't count the muddy ruts we near fell into on the road."

"I wasn't expecting you so soon. I thought you were coming tomorrow." Stephen poured the man a cup of steaming coffee that he always kept on the stove. "Mr. Olney is *The Liberator* agent for Norwich, come to see your brother Charles," Stephen said.

"And Miss Crandall of the infamous school," Mr. Olney said.

"Mary here is a sister of Charles," Stephen said. "And a student at the infamous school."

The man bowed to me, then looked at me carefully. "But I thought all the white students were dismissed," he said.

"I'm not white," I said.

"You are not the color of your brother."

"No." I was embarrassed.

"If you were purple, you would still be an important member of this community as the sister of Charles and a student at that school," he then told me. And when Stephen told him I had been jailed with Miss Crandall he regarded me with open appreciation.

"And you and Stephen are friends then?"

"Yes."

"Stephen is a good man. He is a friend to Negroes."

I thought of the creatures under the floor and nodded.

"He is known far and wide as being a supporter of the school. I hear he sells food when no one else will."

"Yes," I said again. Why did I feel that he was quizzing me, taking my measure?

"Have you had any shipments of java and mocha coffee lately, Stephen?" he asked.

"No," Stephen answered, "but we're expecting one soon."

"And the shipments you have had. Have they been in good order?"

"Perfect."

"And you have been able to dispose of them, then?"

"Every time." Then Stephen smiled at me. "Mr. Olney has some interest in coffee imports," he said.

I nodded, noticing Mr. Olney's shabby shoes. If he had such "interests" I wondered, why did he wear such deplorable shoes? My daddy had told me of merchants in Boston who had a hand in imports and how wealthy they were.

"Does Miss Harris drink coffee?" he asked Stephen.

"She prefers tea," Stephen said. "But I think she could cultivate a taste for coffee if she was given the chance. She has all the qualifications." Qualifications? I scowled at Stephen, angry now that they were talking about me as if I weren't there. Who was this man?

"Perhaps Miss Harris and I could walk together to the school," Mr. Olney suggested. "And I could tell her of the merits of a good cup of coffee."

"Good idea," Stephen said. "Do you mind, Mary?"

I said no and Mr. Olney picked up his bundles and we went out into the drizzling rain. For a while he did not speak, then he told me the bundles were gifts for the school from the office of *The Liberator*.

And a wedding gift for Charles and Mariah. He could not come to the wedding, he said. Then there was more silence and finally he said: "Is she betrothed to Mr. Philleo now?"

At first I was shocked, until I minded that nothing Miss Crandall did anymore was private.

"No. He is away. In Rhode Island. There is no betrothal yet."

"It would be good if there never was one."

I was surprised at the boldness of it. That he, who scarce knew me, would venture to say such a thing. "Why?" I asked cautiously.

"Because he is not a man of good parts. I have heard this from many people."

I drew in my breath. So the rumors about Mr. Philleo were well known, then. There was more to this man than met the eye, I decided. Why was he going out of his way to tell me this?

As if he had read my thoughts, he said, "If you went to jail with her you are close to her, am I right?" he asked.

I said yes, I was.

"Then you should be concerned about Mr. Philleo." He turned to smile at me. He had very white teeth. And his way of speaking was very precise. "You do with this bit of knowledge what you will," he said. "Just make good use of it. Can I trust you to do that?"

Why should he trust me to do anything? Why should I trust him?

"We're both friends of Stephen's," he said, as if he'd heard the questions in my head. "And as such have a lot in common. Stephen attracts only a certain kind of person as friend. And since you are his friend, there is something you should know about Stephen. But you must swear to keep it secret. Can you do that?"

"Quakers don't believe in swearing," I said.

"Are you Quaker?"

"No."

"Then it should not be a problem for you. Unless you do not want to know this thing about Stephen."

Put in that light, of course I wanted to know. "Tell me," I said. "I swear."

"Stephen is an agent on the Railroad." He said it so quietly, so matter of factly, that he might have been remarking on the rain. And for a moment my mind did not lay hold of his meaning. And then it did.

I stared at him. "The creatures under the floor," I said. "And the next day a man came up from the South looking for a runaway."

"You are a clever young woman, Miss Harris. Have you told anyone of your suspicions?"

"No. I've had too much else to think about, I'm afraid."

"And are you in sympathy with what Stephen is doing, then?"

"Of course," I said.

He smiled. "Everyone wonders why a bright young man like Stephen should run a store. That is his reason. People come and go. Shipments come and go. He has food to feed them and contacts."

"Why are you telling me all this now, Mr. Olney?"

"So that if the time ever comes when Stephen needs your help in some way, you will be able to help him. Because Stephen thinks it is time that you know. What say you?"

I felt a thrill of excitement. Here was something to be part of, to stand for, and not just a bunch of selfish silly girls who wanted attention. "How could I help?" I asked.

"Nothing grandiose," he said. "Perhaps just passing a note someday to someone. Giving a signal. Nothing to put you in harm's way. You see, Mary, hereabouts there are a lot of abolitionists. They talk a grand scheme. Oftimes they are the elite. But it is the everyday people, even the poorer ones, who work for the Underground Railroad. There are some in this town."

"Who?"

"That I cannot divulge. I would have to die first, be tortured, put into prison. I cannot name their names. Nor would I give out yours, if you agreed to this. Moreover, you must never ask anyone if they are involved, even if you suspect it."

I wondered about my brother Charles. And Mariah. "I never asked Stephen, and I suspected."

"Good girl. Stephen thought you knew. It's why he trusts you. And another thing. If this thing comes to pass, if you are ever asked to do anything, you must never confide in anyone. You are on your own, except for your instructions. No matter how close anyone is to you, you must never ask for help. Do you understand?"

I said yes. We walked for a while in silence. The rain was abating. "Don't worry," he said. "It may never come to be. You may never be needed. Don't worry the matter any. Think on it good before you say yes."

When we got to the house, I looked at him. "I have decided I could cultivate a taste for coffee, Mr. Olney," I said.

Chapter Twenty-three

Miss Crandall welcomed Mr. Olney at the house. She took the bundles and showed him about. I was asked to take him to the upstairs keeping room where a bright fire blazed, so he could put himself to rights. There we found Amy Fenner, a student, one of the Paines, sewing.

When I introduced her, she gave him a curious look. "We get most suspicious of visitors," she told him.

I thought that most rude. He rubbed his hands in front of the fire and said what a lovely warmth it gave. And how so many of these old houses were drafty, but this one was not. Then he asked her if the problems the town folk had given the school had interrupted the studies. "Oh no," she said.

Mr. Olney took off his wet coat and put it on the back of a chair in front of the hearth. Then he took out his pocket watch and checked it against the time of the clock on the mantel. "That clock is slow," he said. "Perhaps I can come back and fix it later. I like tinkering with clocks."

"Oh that would be wonderful!" Amy said. "It's always been

slow and sometimes makes us late for classes."

We went down for the noon meal and I wondered what she was talking about. No one had ever complained about the clock being slow or making them late for classes.

We ate soup on that chilly fall day. Some of the Paine girls were rudely conferring in the hall and eyeing Mr. Olney. They had to be summoned into the dining room. "What can be so important that you keep our guest waiting?" Miss Crandall scolded.

At the table he spoke politely with the girls, inquiring of each in turn as to their studies. Then he told Miss Crandall about the clock upstairs needing repair, and perhaps while he awaited the arrival of Charles, who was to come this afternoon, he might tinker with it. She agreed. And then, as we were having dessert, he said he had a letter in his coat pocket for Eliza Glasko from her mother.

"Oh!" Eliza squealed. "Can I have it now?"

Yes indeed, she could, he said. And he started to get up. But Amy Fenner said no, she would get it. That he should sit and take his ease. And she ran up to the keeping room. She was such a while up there that dessert was finished when she came back down, and then we all went to class. Mr. Olney went back up to the keeping room to fix the clock.

I was busy with some French verbs about fifteen minutes later when someone yelled, "Fire! Fire! We need an ax!"

It was the voice of Amy Fenner. She was the first one to smell the smoke, to point to the upstairs keeping room. There was a general commotion when she first yelled fire, as one would expect. People scrambled all about. Out in the center hall we spied Mr. Olney on the stairs, his shirtsleeves rolled up, and above his head there was billowing smoke on the landing.

"Water!" Miss Crandall cried. "Water, water, hurry, girls, get the buckets. You know how we've practiced for this!"

We had practiced, passing buckets full of water. Those buckets always sat outside the back door. The girls started toward the door, bumping into each other, some crying. Someone produced an ax, and Mr. Olney took it and ran upstairs again. Miss Almira directed us into a line and we passed the buckets up the stairs. And there was Amy Fenner pushing past the girls in the bucket brigade, up the stairs, yelling, "I left my sewing in that room! The nightgown I was making for Mariah's dowry!"

All was confusion and chaos. "Ring the fire bell!" Miss Crandall's voice came through the smoke from upstairs. Someone dashed outside and across the green to ring it, and soon there were all kinds of people in the house. Men. White men who never ventured near us. Mr. Robinson was there. He was the district schoolteacher and outside were some of his older boys. Downstairs in the first floor parlor was Mr. Chauncy Bacon chopping holes in the walls because, he said, they were hot. Captain Horace Bacon from the Fire Brigade was tearing up floorboards in the parlor. There were muddy footprints all over the place.

After about an hour of this, it was pronounced over. The

fire was out. Captain Bacon said so. "Whoever this man is, he is the hero of the day," he said. And everyone looked at Mr. Olney, but not everyone congratulated him. Some of the men scowled and asked who he was and what he was doing here.

One man asked where the fire had started.

"In the upstairs keeping room," a clear young voice said. It was Amy Fenner. "When Mr. Olney was up there."

There was a lot of conjecture, of course. A lot of discussion. Mariah made coffee and set it up in the kitchen and the men lingered. Classes for the afternoon were called off.

I wandered into the downstairs parlor. And there I found Amy Fenner sitting quietly and gazing out the window. She was smiling.

Within a week the story was in all the newspapers in the Northeast. Reporters came to the house to look around, to see Miss Crandall and talk to the girls. Amy Fenner was interviewed privately and told all she knew of the fire.

Two weeks later Mr. Olney was arrested in a barbershop in Norwich and charged with arson and sent to prison.

I was so confused, I did not know which way to turn inside my head. Had Mr. Olney been arrested because he worked for the Underground Railroad? Or for the fire? I did not believe he had set it, but then, suppose he had?

Why had he come? Should I believe what he had told me? I couldn't even confide in Stephen. He never asked me if Mr. Olney had brought up the matter of the Railroad with me. We never spoke of it, Stephen and I. Never.

Chapter Twenty-four

———⟡———

"**D**id you see the *Hartford Courant?*" Stephen Coit laid the paper flat on the white pine counter in front of me. "It says that Miss Crandall had the fire started."

Miss Crandall? I could not believe it. "What for?"

"To keep up sympathy for her cause. After all, things had died down."

Impossible. Miss Crandall did not resort to such underhanded doings. The Paines, mayhap. The Paines! I tried to make sense of the story in the *Courant*, but could not. My head was spinning.

"Right here." Stephen pointed to the paragraph. "It says that Frederick Olney, as a friend of hers, was brought to start it. The insurance examiner said that someone got down on his or her knees and thrust a lighted taper through a crack between the mopboard and the floor and pushed it along until it fell two inches onto the upper sill of the ground floor window below."

Amy, I thought. Amy Fenner! And the scenes of that day two weeks ago now came before me like pieces in a kaleidoscope. The Paine girls huddling in the hall before our noon meal, eyeing Mr. Olney. Amy begging to be allowed to go up and fetch the letter and taking so long about it. Then Mr. Olney going back to the keeping room after eating to fix the clock and the fire starting.

I felt sick in my stomach.

"And the *Courant* has always defended the school. Are you all right?" Stephen asked me.

I met his kind eyes. How could I tell him? How could I tell anybody of my suspicions? I wanted to confide in Stephen, but something told me not to. Something told me he wouldn't want it, any more than he'd confided in me about his involvement in the Underground Railroad. Our friendship was based, in part, on respect for each other's secrets.

"Yes," I said. "Just a little tired. The whole house is in chaos what with men coming to fix the damage from the fire and getting ready for the weddings."

"Your brother Charles told me that he wants to be a character witness for Olney. So does George Benson. You know the Bensons. Friends of Miss Crandall's?"

"Yes, of course. They are coming to the weddings."

"Think there will be another soon?"

I looked at him. My mind was whirling, thinking about Amy Fenner, but I had to stay becalmed. "I don't know, there might be. Miss Crandall told me that she's heard all the rumors and gossip about Mr. Philleo. And she doesn't believe any of it."

"She said that?" Stephen raised his eyebrows. "To you?"

I blushed. "Ofttime she confides in me," I said. "She is only waiting for him to dispel the rumors," she said.

"Then mayhap someone ought to tell him that," Stephen said.

Well, I decided, it won't be me, but I did not say this. "Miss Crandall feels so betrayed by everyone. She is so disappointed in Mr. Olney. She believes he did start the fire. I think because she does not want to think that someone else in the house may have done it."

"Someone else? But who?"

I blushed. I had said too much. Stephen would not trust me anymore if I said too much. "I cannot say," I told him. I left. On the walk home the anger inside me at the injustice of the arrest of Mr. Olney grew, a hurtful thing choking at me and pushing to get out. I left my basket of produce on the kitchen table without even bothering to say hello to Mrs. Mallard and went to find the Paines. It was Saturday and I found them in Ann Eliza's room, pretending to study.

"How could you?" I burst through the door without knocking.

There were seven of them in the room, sprawled on the bed, sitting on the floor. The fire in the hearth blazed invitingly. There was a tray of tea and cakes. One or two were embroidering. I knew they were still working on a trousseau for Sarah, sewing delicate things, nightgowns. One dressing gown was in pale blue, Sarah's favorite color.

The clothes were strewn on the chair. The newspapers amongst them on the bed. They knew. They had been reading the newspapers and digesting them with their cake and tea. "How could you?" I said again. I directed my accusation at Amy Fenner. "You started that fire, didn't you? When you went up to fetch the letter that day. You did it and you're allowing a good man to wallow in a jail cell for it? How could you stoop so low?"

They pretended surprise, of course. Ann Eliza Hammond got up and defended Amy. "Your accusations are unfounded," she said. "They damage the character of a decent girl. And they endanger us all."

"Endanger?" I flung back at her. "What about Mr. Olney?"

"It has been proven that he did it," said Eliza Glasko.

"Proven? I thought that in this country you are innocent until proven guilty. And who are you saying put him up to it, then? Miss Crandall? As the papers accuse?"

"Don't be silly." Ann Eliza lowered her voice, creating an effect of calm and reason. "He was sent by someone to do it to make it look as if Miss Crandall is looking for publicity. Can't you see?"

"No," I said. "I cannot. I'm sorry. I only see Amy Fenner going up to that room while the rest of us were at our meal. I only remember how long she was up there to fetch a letter. And I only know that I was there before we came down to eat and there was no sign of a fire."

"Because Mr. Olney went up afterward and set it," someone said.

I don't recollect who said it. I only know I went a little daft then, seizing the papers on the bed and throwing them all over, yelling and screaming about a good decent man in jail. Miss Almira and Miss Crandall came running. They had to restrain me. Miss Almira did that, and I remember being surprised at how strong she was as she held my arms tightly behind me.

Miss Crandall said something about being scandalized. About outside publicity not harming her half as much as what was happening to her girls inside.

"Well then," I snapped. "Why don't you open your eyes and tend to it?"

An audible gasp from the girls. Then Miss Almira said something I shall never forgive. "It's what comes from allowing her to be friends with Stephen Coit, sister. He's a troublemaker. What's more, people are talking about their friendship. On several occasions it has come back to me."

And I knew that now I was paying dearly for going against Miss Almira.

"Release her," Miss Crandall said. "We don't use force in this house, sister."

Miss Almira let go of me. And I stood facing Miss Crandall. "Did I not warn you about your friendship with Stephen?" she asked.

"He is a friend, Miss Crandall," I said. "Didn't he help us by asking his father to wait for you and not take the girls away to be whipped?"

"He has been duly thanked and appreciation has been shown. And I have spoken to you about this before, Mary. I told you the problem. I am inclined to think that your rowdy behavior here this morning is the result of Stephen's influence. I am afraid I am going to have to forbid you to see him anymore."

"You can't!" I said.

"Do not tell me what I can and cannot do, please," she said quietly. "You seem to have forgotten all the virtues Plato spoke of. Fortitude, temperance, justice, submissiveness."

"Plato said nothing of submissiveness," I said.

"You are full of sass. What has come over you? Why is Stephen so important? I still have the second part of my trial coming up. People have been talking about you and Stephen, Mary. Exactly the kind of talk I don't need. Remember, one of the foremost fears the town fathers had about this school was the mixing of the races. Remember how they said I would be educating Negro girls who would soon think themselves good enough to marry Canterbury's white bachelors?"

"I'm not going to marry Stephen, Miss Crandall. We're just friends. He's a friend of my family's. How can you forbid me to see him anymore?"

"I can and I must, Mary. I am sorry. You will not make any more trips to the store. You are not to go into town without being accompanied by someone."

"You're just agitated because of everything that's going on."

"I do not let agitation influence my decisions, Mary."

"Well, you are now." And then I said something I shouldn't have said, something people had been saying behind her back. "You're agitated because my sister and Mariah are to wed. And you're not wed, and they're younger than you. And because you've sent Mr. Philleo off because he won't defend himself against all the accusations. And you've invited him to the weddings and don't know if he'll come."

Silence in the room, dreadful silence. Her face went white. She looked about to faint. "How dare you?" she asked. And I knew I had overstepped myself.

"It's what everyone is saying about you. Even your sister. Even the Paines."

"I have befriended you, Mary. You were my best student."

It had a terrible ring about it, like everything was over.

"I am sorry, but I cannot tolerate such behavior. I do not know you anymore. Perhaps I do not know any of my girls anymore. Perhaps things have taken a turn and I will never be able to right them again. I don't know. We all need some time to pray and to think. I shall send a note to your parents. You shall go home this week and do some thinking of your own. And I shall decide if you will come back."

I felt slapped. I was being put out. That was the only word for it. "It's the week before my sister's wedding," I said. "Mama will be busy baking and sewing."

"Go. Pack your things."

Chapter Twenty-five

So I was home again. And the place looked so strange. Smaller than I had seen it before. And shabbier. No center hall, no sweeping staircase, no upstairs keeping room or large sun-filled kitchen. No sound of voices murmuring poetry and no tinkling of pianoforte in the music room. Few books. No need to wear good calico. Homespun would do just fine, thank you, when I fed the chickens or the hogs.

My younger siblings seemed so unlettered. There was no quoting of Plato at the supper table, no discussing Shakespeare. Miss Crandall's second part of her trial had begun and there was no rousing discussion of it over breakfast as the papers were delivered to the door and brought in to be pored over. My room was narrow and poor and Mama was overworked, sewing for the wedding, and making her share of the pumpkin and mincemeat pies and round-bellied puddings speckled with plums.

Everyone worked all the time. I had forgotten the harried

pace, that the cows had to be milked before first light, the pumpkins and last of the corn loaded onto the wagon so Daddy could bring them to market. I had forgotten the smell of manure outside the back doorstep, the cold that froze over in my water bowl in my room even in November.

I felt out of place. Unnecessary. It took me only one day to know I did not belong there. And less time than that for Daddy to tell me that I was not to leave the farm unattended.

I was not to go into town. I was not to see Stephen Coit. Miss Crandall had gotten through to him. "We cannot endanger that school," he told me.

Other than that he and Mama said nothing to me about my abrupt return. At first I tried to help in the kitchen or the farmyard, but I did things wrong. William had things well in hand outside, and the younger girls had grown and were helpmates to Mama in the kitchen.

On the second day Daddy read a letter from Celinda at the breakfast table. In it she expressed her sorrow at not being able to come for the wedding.

"Why can't she come?"

Nobody answered. Except Daddy. "Daughter," he said, "you seem to have forgotten. Celinda is supposed to be in Liberia."

"Still?" I asked. I had forgotten.

"It was published in the African newspapers," Daddy went on quietly. "And because of it other young Negro girls from Windham County have elected to go to Liberia. An understanding about this has been struck with the American Colonization Society."

The understanding struck me, then. For the first time. "You mean Celinda can never come home?"

"Her place at the mill is secure," Daddy said. "As long as we honor our understanding."

"I had an understanding, too, with Mr. Reuben. He said Mr. Hezekiah would always look out for Celinda. That he knows the owners of the mills in Lowell."

"Hezekiah Crandall is a businessman of eminence hereabouts," Daddy said. "Yes, he is friends with other mill owners. But how far do you think he would put his name on the line for a girl of color?"

"Are you saying my understanding with Mr. Reuben means nothing, then?"

"I am saying, daughter, that you already violated that understanding when you went against Miss Crandall and were asked to leave the school. You violated it before he had the chance to."

I flushed. He was right, I had. I had promised Mr. Reuben to take care of his sister, to be a friend to her, and I had turned against her. I felt all my footing giving way beneath me. Everyone at the table was looking at me. Oh, I couldn't abide it! I ran from the room. Out into the cold November morning I ran, across the rutted fields without even a cloak to warm me. I ran under the unforgiving November sky with the sound of crows cawing overhead. I had interrupted their nibbling on the last of the cornstalks.

I wanted to run forever. I was so tired of having everything I thought, everything I believed, amount to nothing in the eyes of others. I was brokenhearted about being put out of school, about not being allowed to see Stephen. I ran until my breath was spent, then sat down on a stump in the middle of the field. A little away, beyond a stream and a fence, was the Mallard place, by no means as big as ours, yet snuggled comfortably in the countryside as if it had been there forever.

I watched the smoke curling out of the Mallard house chimney and felt more sadness. I had not even said good-bye to Mrs. Mallard when I left.

From the corner of my eye I saw my father come across the field, my shawl in his hand. He walked slower than I remembered. He seemed just a little more stooped.

"It's cold, daughter," he said, handing the cloak to me.

I looked up at him. Above his head some crows circled, waiting for us to leave so they could nibble on the last of the cornstalks.

He was angry with me. And his quiet anger was worse than anything. "So you think I should have said nothing, then," I demanded, "about what they did to Mr. Olney?"

"We don't know that anybody did anything to Mr. Olney yet," he said. "Not until his trial."

"And you think it's right I shouldn't be friends with Stephen Coit anymore? After all he's done for us?"

He thrust his hands into his pockets and gazed out across the fields. For a moment all that could be heard was the cawing of crows. "You are at her school, daughter," he said. "You must obey your teacher."

"Not when it comes to betraying a friend," I said.

"She has not asked you to betray. She has asked you to leave off a friendship that people will use against her."

I shook my head and drew my shawl around me. "I can't believe you would say this," I said. "How much are we in this family supposed to sacrifice? Look at Celinda, who can't come home now for her sister's wedding. Don't our feelings count?"

"If we want to better ourselves we must sacrifice," he said firmly.

"But to keep quiet when an innocent man goes to jail? To let those girls get away with lighting the fire? To keep Celinda from coming home? To give up a friendship because of, of . . ." My voice trailed off.

"If those who hate her can prove she is fostering friendships between young whites and Negroes she will be judged guilty," he said. "And then the school will close."

"Well, then, maybe it should close!"

"Daughter! You do not mean that!" He was angry.

"Daddy, you don't know what goes on there. People think it is all goodness and harmony and humility. Well, it isn't. The girls are divided against each other. They fight, they bicker, they connive, they lie."

"That is the way of humans, be they Negro or white, educated or not."

"Miss Crandall preaches humility, but they are all vain and proud. And so is she!"

"Enough, daughter!" He seldom spoke in such a tone. When he did my bones shivered, and not from the cold. We stayed a while in silence. He seemed to be ruminating.

"Daddy," I said. "I don't think I want to go back."

"You will go back," he said. "If she will have you." And then he walked back to the house leaving me there with the crows.

He had no idea, of course. To him I was just a naughty little girl who had sassed her teacher and been sent home to stew about it for a time. To him sassing a teacher was the worst sin possible. Because he had no education.

And because I did, because I went to that school, I knew the difference. I knew the wrongs where he saw none. That was the difference between me and my father that morning. He thought that education in Miss Crandall's school was the gift of a lifetime for his two daughters. I think he would have sent me to Liberia before I could endanger the place.

And because I had the education I knew the wrongs had to be stopped. But I did not see yet that I was the one to stop them.

That night the family went to bed early. Everyone was exhausted with baking and sewing for the wedding. I sat up late by the hearth in the kitchen, reading. Reading had become a habit with me, and I had brought home all my books. Besides, I enjoyed my privacy, another habit I had learned at the school. Miss Crandall had always made sure we had our quiet hour every day. And truth to tell, the bustle and noise of the house was starting to jar my nerves. So I was sitting with my Shakespeare at the fire with a robe wrapped around me, enjoying the quiet, when the soft knock came on the back door.

For a moment I could scarce hear it. Then it came again. I got up and went to look out the kitchen window. A few snowflakes were flurrying outside. Who could it be at this hour? Why, it must be near ten. I could see the man on the porch. Mr. Mallard. Immediately I went to the door. He stood there, casting his eyes to the right of him, then the left, like a man pursued. "Mary," he whispered, "so you are home as my wife said."

"Mr. Mallard, come in. What can I do for you? Shall I fetch my father?"

"No, lass, no. Fetch no one. And I can't come in. And I cannot stay but a minute. My Mrs., she told me it was to you I should give the message. And no one else."

"What message?" Was something wrong at school? Had his wife taken ill? He was a short barrel of a man with graying eyebrows and hair and a face so black I saw him as part of the night.

But when he looked at me with those yellow-brown eyes I saw a fire in them.

"The message is for Stephen. Tell him my shipment has just arrived and must be fetched this night before it spoils."

I knew then, of course. *But the Mallards.* Of all people! Then I remembered what Mr. Olney had said. "It is the everyday people, even the poorer people, who work for the Underground Railroad."

My mind whirled, like the snowflakes above Mr. Mallard's head. But I gathered it in. "The store will be closed now," I said.

"Yes." He nodded. "But he will be back later tonight. All you need do is leave a note under the front doormat on the porch of the store. Say, 'Stephen, the shipment has come.' That is all. Even if someone finds it, no suspicion will be cast. He is waiting for word from me about the shipment. But right now I have a mare down sick and must see to the storage and care of the shipment, and can't go. And Stephen has the means, early in the morning, to send it on to its destination."

"I see." I had no idea this is how it would be, what I had agreed to with Mr. Olney. I had no idea it would come so unexpectedly, so quietly, so unheralded. A soft knock on the door at night from a man I'd known all my life.

But I had promised. And I would keep my word. "I shall get word to Stephen," I promised. "Immediately. Go home, Mr. Mallard. Don't endanger yourself."

"Good, good." He nodded vigorously. "My wife told me you were a good girl. God bless you, child." And with that he turned and went to become part of the dark, swirling night.

When the door closed I stood there for a moment, the

inside of my head spinning. I must gather my wits, I knew. I must act. I had been selected for a moment like this because I was perceived to be trustworthy and smart. What to do first?

Get dressed warm. I did that. I put on my warmest outer clothing. Get a lantern. Write the note for Stephen. Just one line. I set about my business and was just penning the note at the table. *Dear Stephen*, I wrote. Then my father came into the kitchen.

"What's amiss, daughter? Where are you going?"

I stared at him as if he'd just grown horns. He wasn't supposed to be here, he was supposed to be in bed. But he was still fully dressed. Had he been spying on me? I opened my mouth to speak, but no words came.

"Daughter?"

I hastily crumbled the note and held it behind me. "I was just leaving a note for you and Mama when I heard some noise in the barn that sounds like an animal in distress. I was just going to see."

He nodded, came toward me and held his hand out for the note. There was nothing for it but to hand it over. He unraveled it and read the message, then looked at me.

"You were not going to the barn," he said. "This is for Stephen. You were going to leave a note for him at the store. Perhaps see him. Is this not so?"

I was caught. Trapped. The helpless feeling made me weak. Inside me something thrashed, wanted to be let out. "Daddy," I said.

"You were told to stay away from Stephen Coit and now you

are planning to sneak out at this time of night? Have you no shame? You disobey not only your teacher, but us. Daughter, what has happened to you?"

I wanted to tell him. I wanted so badly to tell him. I was surprised he did not hear my heart crying the words out inside me. *Daddy, I'm helping on the Underground Railroad!*

Then I heard my sister Sarah's words: *There is something you don't know about our daddy, Mary. He will do anything not to cause trouble. He will never take a stand for our race.*

And I heard Mr. Olney's words, too: *No matter how close anyone is to you, you must never ask for help. Do you understand?*

I understood. I was on my own.

"I asked what has happened to you, daughter. Will you give no reply? What am I to think, with you running out of the house this time of night to rendezvous with Stephen?"

I could see the disappointment in his eyes, his face. So that was what he thought. Well, I could not disabuse him of his suspicions. I must not.

He crumpled up the note and put it into the fire. "Go to bed, daughter. Now. And don't try sneaking out. I shall sit up all night, if need be. And if need be I shall go against all my own rules and take a horsewhip to you if you disobey. Go!"

I went to my room. But I did not go to bed. I sat on it in the dark, thinking. There was nothing I could do! I was trapped here. My father would hear if I so much as opened a window or walked across the floorboards.

Oh God, I thought, dear God. What will happen to the

shipment if it is not at Stephen's store tonight? If it is not ready for transporting in the morning? I remembered the Southern overseer who had come that time to Miss Crandall's with the sheriff, looking for Cato the runaway.

What happened if they didn't get sent on their way at the appointed time? Would they be caught?

I lay back on my bed, trembling, looking out the window at the snow, which was becoming thicker and thicker. If only, I thought, I hadn't been forbidden to see Stephen. If only Miss Almira had not put such thoughts in her sister's head. If only I had kept my mouth still that day and not attacked the Paines. The message would likely have come to me at school, through Mrs. Mallard. And I'd have been able to sneak out of there so easily.

But now I was here. I couldn't change what had happened, I simply had to make the best of it. It was so quiet out in the kitchen. Was he still there? I opened my door a crack and peeked out. He was sitting in the chair by the hearth where I'd sat earlier. Rocking. His head was tilted to one side, resting, but his eyes were open. I would wait, I decided. He had worked hard all day, he would soon fall asleep, and then I would take my chances.

So I closed my door and waited some more. It seemed like an eternity of hours passed across the darkened sky as I gazed out at my window watching the swirling snow. How far was it to town? Not but two miles. I could make it if I hurried. But he must go to sleep. Please, God, I prayed, make him go to sleep.

It was not the kind of prayer Miss Crandall had ever taught us.

The clock on the kitchen hearth mantel struck midnight. I got up quietly and opened my door again. No sound in the kitchen but the crackling of the fire, the gentle tapping of some snow on the windowpanes, and my father's snoring. He was asleep.

I threw on my coat and hat. I had penned a new note to Stephen while waiting. Gently I pushed up the window sash and climbed out. A lantern! Oh, I needed a lantern. I climbed back in again and took up the lantern, which had been burning on the table when I wrote the note. Outside I set it down on the ground and lowered the window sash. It was snowing seriously now. I took up my lantern and ran.

Chapter Twenty-six

How strange to be out at night alone, trudging across frozen fields with no one about. I was afraid of only one thing, that my father would wake and discover I was gone. I kept looking over my shoulder back to our house, which sat snug with darkened windows, the only sign that anyone lived there being the smoke from the chimney.

I got across our fields and started down the road to town. I knew the landmarks. I could make out certain trees, the bridge over the creek, a few farmhouses. There was no moon, but my lantern gave sufficient light. No windows had lights shining from them. Everyone was abed. A couple of dogs barked at me as I passed, but dogs will bark at a raccoon.

I hurried. It was cold and I drew my coat around me good. The snow was starting to stick to the ground and I supposed I'd leave footprints in it on the way back. I walked on and on. Forever, it seemed, praying, oh please, let me be on time, let me get there in time to give Stephen the note.

It was getting colder, the wind picking up with a bite that froze my toes and fingers. I had to shift the lantern from one hand to another and take off my mittens to blow on my fingers and warm them again. Finally, I saw the outline of the buildings in town. Finally there was a wooded walk under my feet. The storefronts, all deserted, seemed haunted at night. Signs swung and creaked in the wind.

There was no light in Stephen's store. I paused on the front porch scarce believing I was here. There was the mat where I was to leave the note. I set the lantern down, looked around me, but saw no one. I took the note from my pocket and slipped it under the mat.

I wished I could have written something else on the note. Something like "Good luck, Stephen." I wished I could have signed my name, but I knew that was against the rules. I wished I could go inside for a moment and warm myself by his Franklin stove. But I knew I had to get back.

Then, just as I straightened myself up and pulled my muffler around me tighter I saw it. A light in the store! A lantern! Stephen was here! Waiting for the note! Oh, Stephen! I started toward the door, then stopped! He was holding the lantern high and waving it gently back and forth. I stood watching for a moment. And then I knew.

He was thanking me and telling me to go all at the same time.

Tears came to my eyes and my heart filled with such love and a sense of warmth as I have never known. I held up my own lantern, swung it back and forth, and then turned and fled.

I near ran all the way home, filled with a sense of accomplishment that fair gave wings to my booted feet. I had done something good here, something worthwhile, something better than anything my sister Sarah, the Paines, or even Miss Crandall had done.

Tomorrow morning, because of me, a runaway Negro would be on his way to freedom. I knew that for the rest of my life, no matter what happened, I would never forget this night. Because of me the man in Mr. Mallard's house would live a life without fear, be able to make a home somewhere, maybe a family.

Or the woman. Suppose it was a woman? Shivering and half-naked and frightened out of her wits after having come so far from home. Waiting to be delivered out of bondage. Suppose it was a man and a woman and they had a child with them? Mayhap I had saved a whole family!

With all his writing Mr. Garrison had never done that. Nor had Reverend May with all his preaching. I flew across our fields to the house.

And there he was. My father. Waiting for me. Outside my window, the window I had climbed out of. In the cold. In his hand he had a whip, the kind he used on the plow horses in the field.

❋   ❋   ❋

He said nothing except, "Put down the lantern and take off your coat."

I stood there dumb-like. I'd never been whipped. I thought of Julia and the scars on her back. I thought of how she'd said, "No one will ever whip me again. If they do, I'll kill them."

"Do as I say!" he bellowed.

This was not my father. This was not the man I'd always known, who'd held me on his lap when I was a child and told stories, who'd advised and comforted me. Or was he? Mayhap this was my father and I hadn't known him all along. He came at me. He knocked the lantern from my hand. It went rolling on the frozen ground. He tore the coat off me. It was a blanket coat and it wouldn't come off one arm, and he just kept pulling at it and whirling me around and pulling until it did. With the last whirl I fell and he pinned me there to the ground with his foot on my shoulder and my face in the frozen dirt and he hit me with his long and ugly whip. And with every strike, words were pulled from him, from deep inside him.

"Gave you an education and you don't appreciate it." Oh God, my back.

"Turned into an ingrate." Again my back.

"Your mother works twice as hard without you around to help, so you can go to that school." My legs now, oh the pain.

"You don't know how much I wanted an education!" Twice across my buttocks. Oh God, he was killing me.

I yelled. I screamed, I fought, but his foot stayed planted firm, first on my shoulder, then in the middle of my back, hurting more than the lash. "Stop," I yelled. "Stop. I haven't done anything wrong."

"Run off against my wishes to meet with a white man! Endanger your school." It seemed as if the lash was coming with each word now.

Never had I known such pain. It bit into me, it carved itself into me, not only my body but my heart. I thought wildly of Julia. I understood why she wanted to kill anyone who would do such to her again. Then, oh God, then I heard Mama's voice. "Husband, what are you doing! Stop!"

I was told later by Olive, who came running out with her, that she had to throw herself against him to make him stop. And that when he did, he looked at her wild-eyed, drew back his whip, and made as if to hit her with it, too. "Act like a nigra she gets treated like one," he said. That's what Olive told me later.

I huddled on the ground, burning all over. I huddled against the cold earth for comfort. I would have dug my way into it if I could have. It gave me more understanding, more welcome, than I could ever expect from my own father.

Somehow, Mama becalmed him, got him into the house, directed Olive to help me. Lights were on inside now, piercing the night. I saw my brother William, the little ones cowering in there, fear big on their faces. Olive brought me into the kitchen and sat me down. Mama led my father into their bedroom and I heard her scolding him there. I heard words like "never" and "cruelty" and "no call to do such" and "ashamed" and "abomination." Then it got quiet and Mama came out to tend to me. She directed Olive to get things, salve, warm water, rags, even brandy.

I shivered and was hot and cold all at the same time. My teeth were chattering. I could not make them stop. My face was scraped where I'd hit the ground, my shoulder and back bruised where he'd set his boot upon me. My whole body shook. Mama's words turned soothing now, like her hands, like the remedies she put on me. But I cried and couldn't stop crying until she held me.

And then I told her. "I hate him," I said.

"Hush, he's your father."

"What does that mean? Does that wash it away? He had no right. I did nothing wrong, Mama, I swear it."

"I know, child, I know, but you were put out of school and he wants you to be able to go back. And he doesn't want anything to ruin that."

"I hate that school. I hate Miss Crandall. This is all her fault. We've been friends with Stephen all our lives. Doesn't that mean anything to Daddy at all?"

She held me until I quieted. She gave me something to make me sleep. I went to bed that night muddled in my head, half out of it. But the half I was in knew, remembered, what I'd done that night. And knew it was good and it was right. But I couldn't rightly recollect why.

I fell asleep and awoke the next morning to a blue bowl of a sky, sunshine, and a sugarcoating of snow on the ground. I awoke hurting, and at first I could not remember why.

Then I did. And the remembering was a mixed business, joy at what I'd done, and wonder at how, even now, the shipment of coffee was finding its way out of Canterbury. And sorrow at what my father had done to me.

Sorrow and anger and even hatred. How could I live in this house? I tried to get up, but my shoulder and back ached so I felt as old as Mr. Mallard. And then Olive came in, sent by Mama, to help me dress.

"You're going back to school today," she said.

"Who said?"

"Ma said. A note came from Miss Crandall, saying you should come back. That she needs you."

I didn't want to go back. I didn't feel I could live there, either, after what she'd done to me. But I could live there easier than I could live here.

"Ma says you're to put on your second-best dress."

"I don't want to see Daddy at breakfast."

"No need to worry about that. He's with the boys in the barn. I don't think he wants to see you, either. Ma says he's ashamed of himself."

Whether those words held true, I didn't know. But he wasn't at breakfast. Mama made me eat and fussed over me. She showed me the note from Miss Crandall. "There, now that ought to make you feel better, doesn't it?"

It didn't. But I didn't press Mama. After breakfast Olive helped me get my things together. Daddy had come in now. I heard him in the kitchen with Mama. They were gathering the cakes and pies she had baked for the weddings, bringing them out to the wagon.

I hated even riding in the wagon with my father back to the school. But there was no way out of it. I busied myself packing. Mama had made me a new dress for Sarah's wedding. It had a lace collar, but was not too fancy. I made up my mind that it would be perfect for my trip to Lowell. In back of my mind a plan was forming to soon go there. I knew I wouldn't finish out at the seminary.

I knew, too, that I would probably not be coming home again. I'd stay at Mariah and Charles's house on holidays. They were renting a small house close to the school. So I took all my treasures, my childhood rag doll, the brooch Mama had given me when I turned thirteen that had been hers as a child, even my collection of bird feathers.

Olive was watching me. "Why are you taking those things?"

I did not answer. I loved Olive, but I felt years and years older than her, like we had no common ground anymore.

On the ride back to school Daddy didn't talk to me at all. And it made no nevermind to me. When he pulled the horse to a halt behind the house, he got out and started bringing the pies and cakes into the kitchen. I let him. I didn't offer to help. Mrs. Mallard greeted me as if she knew nothing about what had happened with her husband and the note last night. I longed to ask her if she knew, but I didn't dare.

Right off, of course, she saw me walking like an old lady.

"What happened?" she whispered.

I just shook my head and told her I had fallen.

When he brought in the last of the pies and cakes, Daddy looked at me. "Mind yourself," he said. "This is your last chance for an education." He did not put an arm around me or kiss me, or even say good-bye. I watched him go out the door.

Mind yourself, I said in my head. I stood watching him get into the wagon, snap the reins and start off, wishing I might never see him again. But I would have to, at the wedding. I knew I should feel something, but I didn't.

Then I felt a hand on my arm and turned. Mrs. Mallard looked into my face. "It will be all right," she said. "You are a good girl. I always told my husband that."

That was how she told me that she knew about the note. And that the shipment had gotten off all right. I went into the house proper, feeling lots better about things.

There was an argument going on. It was like I'd never left. Did these girls never move beyond their own selfish concerns? They sounded like the crows in the fields. It seems that the Paines wanted to wear their usual black for the weddings. But Miss Crandall said no.

"What about the dresses Mrs. Weldon in the village is making for all of you? Your parents paid dearly for those dresses?"

They agreed to go to town and have a fitting. Sarah and Mariah wanted to go, too. The mood was downright festive.

"I'm so glad you're back." Miss Crandall smiled and opened her arms to me. I went to her. "I hope you will forget our recent disagreement. We have all been under a strain. It means nothing. We Quakers believe in forgiveness."

Did she mean she was forgiving me? I didn't push it. My shoulder and back, everything hurt when she embraced me. I had all I could do to keep from crying out. I drew away from her. No, she didn't know about the Underground Railroad, but leaving that out, didn't she know what her edict about Stephen had cost me? I watched as she gathered the girls around her and they put on their bonnets.

"Oh, Mary, I forgot." She turned to me. "It's up to you to hold down the fort this afternoon. I've given Mrs. Mallard the afternoon off. Poor dear needs a rest. If, by any means, Mr. Philleo comes by, tell him we'll be back by four. Not that I'm expecting him, mind you. Enjoy your solitude. I wish I had it for an afternoon."

She was expecting Mr. Philleo. That was the reason for her gaiety. I watched her in a stupor as they went out the door. I felt so removed from them all, so outside the circle of them. Why had I never seen them all the way I was seeing them now?

And her. I had always considered her the highest form of being, above us all, possessed by some spirit of piety and goodness. But she could be just as silly, just as vulnerable, as anyone else.

I was glad I was going to be alone this afternoon. Inside me thoughts were gathering, like crows in the cornfield, one after another, coming to settle and peck. I needed to make sense of them.

Chapter Twenty-seven

———◦◦◦———

When Mrs. Mallard had taken her leave I wandered about the house as if I had never seen it before. It was sparkling clean, though the egg-stained curtains in the dining room still hung, still besplattered, like some kind of battle flag. The rock that had come through the window was still on the mantel. But all the damage had been repaired.

The wood floors gleamed. The house smelled of fresh baking. In the kitchen I arranged all of Mama's offerings. I supposed I should be happy about my sister getting married, but I felt more kinship with Mariah. In spite of my hurts, I paced, my mind forming thoughts into a plan, a plan of what I would do if Mr. Philleo came.

Stephen had given me the idea without knowing it. Yet I supposed it was there, inside me all along.

I had to answer the front door knocker three times and accept packages that came for Mariah and Sarah. It seemed like everyone in the world knew about their weddings. Because of Miss Crandall.

Well, I thought, that's what Sarah had wanted, anyway. And then I thought how the weddings would probably be in all the newspapers. I was not envious, no. I could not waste time on such feelings. My every nerve, all the blood pounding in my veins directed my thoughts at Miss Crandall.

What did she think I was, anyway, a flit of a girl to be toyed with? Did she think I wanted to come back here? Did she not understand that the things I had learned here had only made me critical of her? Her experiment had succeeded, yes. She had proved that Negro girls could learn. But did she think it went only so far? And then we could be ordered about like trained dogs?

I thought of all the fame she had acquired on account of this school. And then I thought about Stephen inside his store last night, waving that lantern, like a beacon at me, back and forth. And never asking credit for what he was doing. Never wanting anyone to know.

And I hated her. It had nothing to do at all with what I'd suffered at my father's hands, though she was to blame for that, too. I just hated her. She was what the papers said, a pawn of the abolitionists. They were using her, and she didn't even know it.

And she was using us. Well, I thought, not me. She is not using me. And then suddenly, it all came together for me. And I knew what I would do.

I was just about to go upstairs and get a book from my room

when the front door knocker sounded again. I went to answer it. He stood there, wearing a gray broadcloth suit and a fancy blue cravat, his hat in his hand. "Hello, Miss Mary," he said. "It is Miss Mary, isn't it? Is your mistress home?"

The shock of him standing there took me aback for a moment. Had I conjured him with my thoughts? It was too good to be true. "She isn't my mistress," I said. "She's my teacher."

He shrugged. "Is she home?"

"No. They've all gone to town to see to the dresses for the wedding." I looked beyond him and breathed easier not to see his obnoxious daughter. "Won't you come in, Mr. Philleo? I'm sure she'll be home directly."

I knew that if I were to do what I wanted to do it had best be now. It might be my one and only chance.

He had a small gift. It looked like a book. He came in and handed it to me, took off his coat, and I set it and his hat aside. "There's a bright fire in the front parlor. Would you like some tea?"

He said yes, tea would be nice. He had come a long way. He had come for the weddings, he said. "If Miss Crandall will have me."

It sounded as if he were going to say the wedding vows himself. I fetched the tea quickly, trying to keep myself becalmed. I brought it to the parlor and set it down. "Have you come on an extended visit this time, Mr. Philleo?" I asked.

He settled back on the settee. "This is nice," he said,

looking around the room, which was bright with sunshine. "Yes, this is very nice." He spoke as if he was deciding to buy the house. Or acquire it, I thought. Because the way the laws are, if he married her, he'd come into possession of it all. All her property.

"I'm sure Miss Crandall will be happy to see you," I said. "She was hoping you would come."

"Was she?" He sipped his tea.

"Yes. She told me just the other day she was hoping you would come."

His eyes narrowed as he set down his cup. His long sallow face had deep creases. (How old was he? Forty-six, Miss Crandall had said.) He studied me and his preacher's eyes took in everything about me. I am sure he thought he could see through to my soul. Preachers always think they can. But if he had known what was in my soul at this moment, he would have run from me like I was a burning bush. Or may-hap he wouldn't have. I sat, steadfast, before him.

"Has she missed me, then?" he asked. "Has she said she missed me? You are her confidante. That is what we all hear. Could you help a lovestruck man and tell him what his chances are?"

I shall remember my answer to this day. I shall remember it always. I had, after all, a long time to remember it. Many was the morning in the mill, as I learned to thread the loom, as my ears and head pounded from the noise, as I stood in shoes that held swollen feet, that I wished I had not said it. But I did.

"Mr. Philleo," I said.

"Reverend," he corrected. "It's Reverend Philleo, child."

"Reverend," and I prayed inside that God would forgive me for calling him such, "Reverend, may I be forthright?"

"I would consider it an honor."

"Well, Reverend, forgive me for seeming bold. But we have all heard the rumors about you." His eyes narrowed. Was he moved to anger? Would he accept this from me? And then I saw the look in his eyes, the eagerness, the hunger, the greed. It was the greed that surprised me. I had never before seen it, so naked, in anyone's eyes.

"Reverend," I said, "Miss Crandall does not believe the rumors. She told me so herself. But she also told me that she is waiting, just waiting, for you to come to your own defense."

A light came into his eyes then. I don't know what it was. I suppose I was still too young to recognize it.

"She is?"

"Oh yes, sir. Why she was crying over the matter the other day. Said how she held you in such high esteem and missed you so, and was just waiting for you to speak up and defend yourself. Only. . ." I hesitated.

He leaned forward. "Only what?"

"Only you mustn't tell her I told you this, Reverend, sir. Because she'd be dreadful angry with me. And because it would ruin it for her if she thought you had to be encouraged to defend yourself. But I know how highly you think of each

233

other and so I just had to speak my mind. You will forgive me if I've overstepped myself. Won't you, sir?"

He slapped his knee with his hand. He whooped in a most unreverend like manner. "I knew it!" he said. "I just knew it." He stood up. He paced. He could not contain himself, it seemed.

"I should go," he said. "I should make my entrance later. Then she'll have no suspicion you even saw me."

I thought that a good idea and told him so. I saw him out the door. I handed him his hat. And after he had left I closed the door and stood leaning against it and the silence of the grand old house mocked me. Soon, I thought, soon there will be no more pianoforte tinkling in the other room, no more baking smells from the kitchen, no more recitations of poetry, no more globes of the world sitting around, no more quill pens and bottles of ink and girls' laughter.

For one terror-stricken moment I was frightened at what I had done. Could one person effect such a change? When others, so many powerful others had tried and failed? But I knew the answer. Yes. Especially if that one person was regarded like a shadow, with her name never to go in the newspapers or court records, a comfortable shadow kept around just to fetch things, to tell things to, a shadow to be told who she could and couldn't be friends with. But then how will I ever come out of the shadows? I thought. If this school was not the way, then what is?

I did not have the answer for that. I remembered how once Miss Crandall had told us that all answers did nothing more than pose new questions. But that every question answered was another door open. And that was what learning was all about.

And now, for me, there would be no more questions. I had run out. Now, for me, there would be no more opened doors.

Chapter Twenty-eight

They were wed on August 12 in the next year. By then Miss Crandall's trial was over. It went on all spring and Mr. Philleo kept going to the courthouse in his blue cravat. His daughter, thankfully, did not come to Canterbury.

In the end everybody lost, even though Miss Crandall was not convicted. She was let off the hook, my brother Charles told me, by a technicality. It seemed that the first warrant for her arrest charged her wrong. It said she was charged with "harboring and boarding colored persons, not inhabitants of this state, without license, for the purpose of being instructed."

The judge said all this meant was that she was running a boardinghouse with no license, and the object of the legislation was to regulate unlicensed schools, not unlicensed boardinghouses.

The law can do wonderful things when it wants to. But the abolitionists, who all the time wanted to take Miss Crandall's case to the Supreme Court, where it would be decided once and for all if we Negroes were citizens, were disappointed.

It was over.

The wedding almost didn't happen, though. I don't know why Miss Crandall wanted to be wed at the Congregational Church on the green, when the congregation would never take in her Negro girls to worship. Reverend Otis Whiton, who was new there, published the bans and said he would marry them. But while we all waited in the front parlor of the house, he sent a note around saying he was sick.

Later Mariah found out he had been given an envelope with a good deal of money for the church if he did not perform the ceremony. So we all had to get in carriages and go over to Brooklyn. The Bensons came. Even Henry. But I managed to avoid him.

By the time Miss Crandall wed, both Mariah and Sarah were expecting babies. I stayed on at the seminary after the wedding. Nothing happened for a while and it seemed as if everything would settle down and the school would go on. When Reverend and Mrs. Philleo returned from their wedding trip, piles of gifts awaited them from around the world. By that time there was another stone on the mantel, which had been thrown through the window while she was away.

We girls were instructed to call her Mrs. Philleo now instead of Miss Crandall. It did not seem proper somehow. The name did not fit.

Mr. Philleo (in my head I called him that, not Reverend) settled in. He soon had turned the upstairs keeping room, where the fire had been, into his own study.

The March before they married, Mr. Olney had been acquitted of arson.

Mr. Philleo also took over more than the keeping room. He took over the running of the school. He went over the accounts himself now. Miss Crandall had recently given them to Miss Almira to do. Miss Almira left in a huff and went to live with her father. Because you don't ever take anything away from Miss Almira.

The school was spending too much money, Mr. Philleo said. And so he did away with afternoon tea, which everyone looked forward to after classes and before study time. Especially on cold spring afternoons. He stopped the account with Stephen Coit's store.

In the months that followed the wedding I did not go home again, though Olive came to the school and begged me to. I went, instead, to Mariah and Charles's house. Charles had been told what Daddy had done to me. And, as it turned out, Charles knew why.

Mariah and Charles were also involved in the Underground Railroad in Canterbury, though they never spoke of it. And Charles spoke of it only that once to me, when he said of Daddy: "He would never understand. You did well not to confide in him, though you suffered his wrath. You can come here any time you want, Mary."

I saw Stephen once or twice in the months that followed. When I did it was at Mariah and Charles's house. Right next door to the seminary. Right under Mrs. Philleo's nose. And again, we never spoke of that night at all.

Celinda never came home again. At Christmas I got a note from Julia Williams. She was happily attending a school for Negro women in Boston. She hoped to someday teach at the Noyes Academy in New Hampshire. "Come to school here in Boston," she begged, "as soon as you can."

I talked it over with Mariah and Charles. We decided I would stay in the seminary as long as I could, then go to the mill with Celinda for a while to earn some money so I could be independent. "It would take several months," Charles figured, "and then with some money I can give you, you can go to Boston." So I made plans. And the days at the seminary were made bearable.

After Miss Crandall and Mr. Philleo were married, it was just a matter of watching the school fall apart. Gradually he took away all our amenities. There would be no new books, no new musical instruments. If we all did chores there would be no need to hire a woman to clean.

Everyone hated him. Especially the Paines. Because as soon as he discovered their activity he made Mrs. Philleo order them to stop wearing their black dresses and meeting in secret. Some of them immediately left, dwindling the income from tuition.

Everyone in town loved him. He went about sporting, going

to Freemason Meetings and political gatherings, and receiving newspaper reporters. He had a private sale in town of many of the gifts that came for Mrs. Philleo from around the world. Even the Staffordshire plates.

He made his wife go on visits with him to preach. To Boston, to Philadelphia. Mariah and Sarah took over the teaching. More girls left. I stayed, getting all the learning I could. When she was home, I stayed away from Mrs. Philleo. It was not the same anymore between us.

The September after the Philleos wed, Sarah had a baby girl. She named her Prudence Crandall Fayerweather. The event brought me and Sarah together again, because I sewed many new clothes for the new arrival. But our feelings for one another would never be as they had been before.

I came home to the seminary late that night from Sarah and George's place just outside town. George drove me back. I went to sleep promptly, at some measure of peace with myself. But not for long. Because late that night the school was attacked with no provocation at all. It was attacked by a band of men. They beat the doors and windows with lead pipes. They tore out what windows they could not smash. In back of the house on the ground floor a room had been made up for two students, because Mr. Philleo wanted his own dressing room upstairs. The band of men broke into that room and one of the girls was so frightened she went into hysterics and could not be calmed.

They came into the house and destroyed furniture and

knocked over bookcases and lamps. It took Mr. Philleo a good fifteen minutes to come downstairs. First he had to get fully dressed, even to his blue cravat. My brother Charles was there before him, trying to stop the mayhem.

The next day five more girls went home. Mrs. Philleo stayed in seclusion. She would not even see her father when he came.

"Where is my daughter?" he asked me.

"She is not available to receive anyone," I told him.

Mr. Pardon looked around at the destruction and nodded. "She is gone," he said. And then he left. I knew what he meant. She had been gone from that place for a long time.

The next day there was no school. Mr. Philleo put notices in *The Unionist* and in *The Liberator* that the house was for sale and the school was closed.

They had been married less than a month.

Everyone said it closed because of the final attack. But I know it closed the day Miss Crandall married Mr. Philleo. I know what I did. And I am not sorry.

Before I left I went upstairs to Mrs. Philleo's room and stood in the doorway. She was at her desk, writing. She looked up. "Yes?"

"I'm leaving, Mrs. Philleo."

"Yes, well have a good trip." Her eyes were red from crying. She seemed in a daze. I think she did not recollect who I was.

I left with the blessing of Charles and Mariah and Mrs.

Mallard. I left without telling Sarah, not because I was angry with her, I had long since gotten over that. But because I knew she would have told Mama. And I knew I could not be strong against Mama's plea that I stay.

There was, somehow, a peace inside me when I left. Yet at the same time, every so often there was an emptiness that could not be filled. I worried about Mama and how she would take my leaving. Charles said he would tell Mama. He would make it all right with her.

I was at the mill for a while before I began to understand that you can find a cause anywhere if you are looking for one. Celinda was very much a part of working for justice for the mill workers who are treated near as bad as some of the slaves in the South. She has asked me for my help.

I have told her I cannot take such chances, I who ran out in the night to deliver a message to Stephen and earned myself a whipping for it. I have told her I must not lose my position, for I must save my money so I can go to school in Boston. So she has given me little things to do, like pass messages to the girls about some meeting. Nothing dangerous. I'm not saying I believe in what she's doing. I'm only saying I'm helping.

The work here at the mill is hard, and betimes I conclude that I will never be able to do it. But then I think of that man or woman huddled in Mr. Mallard's house, who had come so far and dwelt for the moment in darkness and fear. And I think what I did then to help him or her. Or them. And what

I withstood after. And I know we can do anything if we set our minds to it, and believe in what we are doing.

And I suppose, in the end, that's what my sister Sarah meant. Strange, it is her words that come back to me more than anybody's now.

"You've got to believe in something."

Author's Note

I came upon the story of Prudence Crandall while researching another novel. The idea intrigued me, but once I began the research certain things about the story did not add up. Or rather, there were many questions that still were unanswered.

For instance, in all the research, though thumbnail sketches of the black girls who attended the seminary are given, there is nothing written about what their disposition was once they were inside its walls. How did they interract, one with another? How did they respond to the problems the school and Miss Crandall suffered? Were they all modest, retiring, submissive, uncomplaining, long-suffering, and sacrificing? I found this difficult to believe. The only indication I found about their reactions was when Sheriff Roger Coit came to the house to take them away to be whipped. It is written that they were submissive and willing. And that one, Ann Eliza Hammond, had disappointment in her voice when Miss

Crandall came up with the bond to rescue them from this terrible punishment.

As for Miss Crandall herself, research also led me to think that once Prudence Crandall saw the reaction of the people of Canterbury to her first black student, she immediately contacted William Lloyd Garrison, editor of *The Liberator* in Boston.

Taking nothing away from her brave actions and good intentions, it seems that Prudence Crandall knew, at once, what she was on to in championing the rights of blacks and going against the role allotted to women of her time. In today's world, her contacting *The Liberator* would be like contacting the six o'clock news or one of the network morning shows. Indeed, she was often accused in the newspapers of the day of being a pawn or a tool of the abolitionists. And whether she did this to aid her cause, or she could simply not keep the newspapers at bay, is still open to conjecture. It is an unanswered question.

Another one is: Why did Prudence Crandall deliberately antagonize the Board of Visitors, who backed her financially for the initial school for white girls, by not informing them that she was dismissing those girls and opening the school to "little misses of color"? It is a debated fact that if she had gone to the Board of Visitors herself about her plans, instead of letting them find it out from the newspapers, they might have been more lenient with her. And it has been said that their anger at her stemmed as much from this omission as from the fact that she was bringing Negro girls into Canterbury.

It is well known, of course, that Prudence Crandall, long known as an obstinate girl with a penchant for new ideas, was not bothered by breaking new ground and upsetting the establishment. This was part and parcel of her heritage. Her ancestors were malcontents. In 1635 the first Crandall on America's shores was banished to Rhode Island from Massachusetts Bay Colony because he was an Anabaptist. There he did extremely well amongst the other outcasts.

So, if it was time for a school to be opened for black girls in staid old Canterbury, Connecticut, Prudence Crandall was the one to do it, and I could not help applaud her efforts. Yet as a writer I had to deal with the ambiguities I was presented with. And I would be less than honest if I wrote it simply as the story of a devout Quaker woman whose efforts were trampled upon, whose students were malleable and submissive, without the feelings, ambitions, rivalries, or fears of normal teenagers.

I found it difficult to believe that some twenty teenage girls remained silent, unbiased, unafraid, uninvolved, and submissive. These girls were human beings with the same emotions, needs, and potential of everyone else. Isn't that what Prudence Crandall was trying to prove? So there, inside the school, I found my story.

How much is true and how much fiction? Well, all the girls mentioned at the school did attend at the time. Julia Williams did come from South Carolina, and after leaving the school attended the Noyes Academy in Canaan, New Hampshire, where, in August 1835, three hundred armed men with ninety teams of oxen dragged that school building off its foundation. Julia met Henry Highland Garnet there, married him, and they went to the Oneida Institute in Whitesboro, New York, to teach.

Sarah Harris did ask Miss Crandall to attend her school and about her Miss Crandall did say, "The school may sink, but I will not give up Sarah." Sarah wed George Fayerweather. Later they became involved in the antislavery movement and while living in Kingston, Rhode Island, gave refuge to and entertained many activists, such as Frederick Douglas and William Lloyd Garrison.

William Lloyd Garrison and others mentioned as backing and giving moral support to Prudence Crandall actually did so. Mariah was the first black girl to attend classes, sitting on the floor after her chores were finished. She did wed Mary's brother Charles Harris. Stephen Coit was the son of Sheriff Coit and was the only storekeeper who would sell to the school in its time of trouble. The sheriff did come to the house to take the girls away to be whipped and Prudence Crandall did post bond to stop it. Accordingly, Pardon Crandall was just as I have him in the novel, as were Prudence's brothers, Hezekiah and Reuben Crandall.

There was an Underground Railroad active in Canterbury. As for our protagonist, Mary Harris, she did attend the school with her sister. I have brought her to life and given her the role she has to further the story. As she was my protagonist, I took liberties with the character of Mary, and the events involving her—one of them being that she accompanied Miss Crandall to jail that one night.

But taking liberties with the minor characters in the historical text is what fiction writing is all about. I've brought them to life by putting words in their mouths in keeping with the boundaries of the history presented. For history, exciting as it is, does not make them three-dimensional, or put emotions in their hearts, or connect the dots in the story. That is the job of the historical novelist. The only characters I had to invent for this story were the Mallards, the overseer from the South, and the runaway slave, Cato, whom he comes seeking. But such a scenario happened often in Canterbury and other Underground Railroad towns.

The school and Miss Crandall were persecuted by the town in exactly the ways I have related, everything from the dead cat to the poisoning of the well. And Miss Crandall responded as I have related, from keeping the egg-stained curtains hanging to putting the rock that came through the window in a place of honor on the mantel. There was a Frederick Olney who came to town to visit Charles Harris and see the school. He was blamed for the fire in the house and Miss Crandall was accused of having it started for publicity.

At the time young white girls were going off in droves to work in the cotton mills. I have Celinda, Mary's sister, going too. The cotton mills were very much a part of the culture at this time in New England, and I had hoped Celinda's letters home would help to bring in another dimension of human suffering, another societal wrong of the time, and balance it against the trials of the girls in the school.

All that is known about Mary's father, William Montiflora Harris, is that he came from the West Indies, that he was a successful farmer, and that he hoped for education for himself, but was intent upon it for his children.

There are frequent instances in the narrative when Prudence has her girls praying. While one may insist that this is not the way of Quaker worship, that Quakers attended meetings where they sat in silence until the spirit moved them to speak, research indicated that Prudence ran her school for girls of all faiths and prayer was part of it.

On page twenty of *Prudence Crandall, a Biography*, by Marvis Olive Welch, we are told, "Always seeking truth in science and religion, she [Prudence] sometimes went to meetings conducted by Baptist speakers in nearby churches, or took trips to nearby churches to hear revivalists."

At some time during the formation of the school, Prudence must have written to her brother Reuben asking about religious services. Welch tells us how Reuben advised her in a letter: "As far as regular religious activities, I will give my consent provided no male is present who can officiate."

I went with this as evidence that Prudence Crandall had prayer meetings in her school for girls of all different faiths, and did not adhere to the Quaker way of silent fellowship.

But this original intention of Miss Crandall's, to open a school for young black girls in a staid old New England town, did not remain as it was intended. There were too many forces at work, politically, at the time. One was the American Colonization Society, whose members were her chief enemies and whose purpose was to solve "the Negro problem" by exporting them all to Liberia. Everyone, it seems, had an ax to grind, a selfish agenda, and hopped on the bandwagon of Miss Crandall's school, especially the Reverend Calvin Philleo, who married Miss Crandall and closed the school within a month of the marriage.

History has him down as not only greedy, but as a womanizer, looking for a wife of property. By the time he met Prudence Crandall her fame was real, not only in America but throughout the world. After her marriage to him, Prudence Crandall was not very happy, and one wonders why she married him when all her friends warned her against the union and he had such a disreputable reputation. However, we must remember that she was already thirty when they met, and in 1833 that marked her as an "old maid." This was not an admirable state in that time. If not married, she would be pitied, looked down upon, and not really considered a part of productive, contemporary society. In short, Philleo was probably her "last chance."

Many young women of the day married for the same reasons. To be without a husband and a family was to be on the lowest rung of the social ladder.

The Philleos never again seemed to have a home after leaving Canterbury. They moved throughout New England, to New York State, then to Illinois. They were childless and had financial troubles because of Philleo's failed business dealings. In 1848 they were living in Illinois, and though the marriage was very unhappy, Prudence Crandall stayed with Calvin Philleo, true to Quaker tradition, although she no longer accepted financial support from him. He died in Illinois in 1874.

After his death Prudence Crandall, now seventy-one, traveled with her brother Hezekiah, who was seventy-seven, to Kansas, to a farming community, but she kept in touch with old friends and family back East and corresponded regularly with nieces and nephews. Historians claim that once Mr. Philleo married her she stopped having anything to do with the abolitionist movement. It makes one wonder if he was not jealous of the eminence she had acquired.

Prudence Crandall Philleo died in January 1890, in her Kansas home. She was eighty-seven. In 1886, Windham County, Connecticut, was a leader in the fight for Negro suffrage, the right for Negroes to vote. Perhaps this was due to the earlier groundwork laid in Canterbury by Prudence Crandall.

Within weeks of his arrest, Frederick Olney was acquitted of arson. In 1844 he married Olive Harris, sister to Mary and Sarah. History does not tell us where Mary Harris went after the school closed. I like to think she joined Julia Williams at the Noyes Academy. Certainly she had further education, because we do know that she married Pelluman Williams, a teacher in Norwich, Connecticut, in 1844. And that after the Civil War they moved to New Orleans, Louisiana, where both taught school. It would be nice to think they taught children who were freed from slavery.

Bibliography

Blockson, Charles L. *The Underground Railroad: Dramatic Firsthand Accounts of Daring Escapes to Freedom.* New York: Berkley Books, 1989.

Dublin, Thomas, ed. *Farm to Factory: Women's Letters, 1830–1860.* New York: Columbia University Press, 1981.

Mayer, Henry. *All on Fire: William Lloyd Garrison and the Abolition of Slavery.* New York: St. Martin's Press, 1998.

Nylander, Jane C. *Our Own Snug Fireside: Images of the New England Home, 1760–s1860.* New York: Alfred A. Knopf, 1993.

Robinson, Harriet H. *Loom and Spindle, or Life Among the Early Mill Girls.* Kailua, Hawaii: Press Pacifica, 1976.

Strane, Susan. *A Whole-Souled Woman: Prudence Crandall and the Education of Black Women.* New York: W. W. Norton & Company, 1990.

Walsh, Jeannine B. "Prudence Crandall: A Clarification of the Canterbury Tale and its Heroine." Abstract from thesis submitted to the Department of History, Southern

Connecticut State College, 1976.

Welch, Marvis Olive. *Prudence Crandall, a Biography.* Manchester, Conn.: Jason Publishers, 1983.

Woodward, Carl R. "A Profile in Dedication, Susan Harris and the Fayerweather Family." *The New England Galaxy,* 15, no. 1 (1973).

Yates, Elizabeth. *Prudence Crandall, Woman of Courage.* Honesdale, Pa.: Boyds Mills Press, 1955.